I0831173

A CUP OF AUTHENTICITEA

A CUP OF AUTHENTICITEA

SHORT STORIES AND REFLECTIONS TO SIP ON WHILE YOU'RE STEEPING.

CHRISTINA OWENS

STINAGENE.

ISBN number 979-8-9990263-0-9
LCCN 2025910774
Printed in the United States of America
First Edition
Credits
Cover and Interior Design: Mindhatch Creative
Author's Photo: James Lee

This book was independently published with the support of several generous individuals from coaching conversations to editing to thoughtful early readers.

Any small imperfections are just part of the blend, like the leaves at the bottom of your cup, reminders that this was made with soul, not mass-produced.

Disclaimer

This book blends memory and metaphor, brewed by the author who lived, listened, and felt deeply enough to pour it all into stories and steeped reflections.

To protect the real people who inspired these pages, all names and identifying details have been changed, because everyone deserves their own cup of peace.

Speaking of cups, this isn't a guide to perfect tea. It's a companion for imperfect moments. The author claims no tea expertise, only a deep love for the ritual and meaning behind every brew. May each sip invite you to slow down, reflect deeply, and seek professional support when needed.

The First Pour Goes To…

My younger self, may you always lean into curiosity, trust your path, and savor each moment as it comes.

And for those who have shared their experiences with me, your openness, wisdom, and authenticity have poured into this book in ways I can never fully express. Thank you!

The Menu

FROM THE COUNTER

Welcome! There's something about *The Authenticitea Café* that makes people pause. It's not just the aroma of steeped herbs or the flicker of light in the window, it's something quieter. Something that asks you to sit with yourself, even for a moment.

This place offers more than tea. It offers what we all need but rarely request: presence.

At the heart of the café is a menu unlike any other: *A Cup of Authenticitea.* Each one prepared with intention. Each one served with a story.

Some guests arrive by chance, drawn in by the glow beyond the glass. Others return often, knowing what awaits within: a question met with calm, a reflection poured with care, and a folded napkin carrying the kind of wisdom that finds you when you're ready.

Inside, time slows. The scent of hibiscus, chamomile, citrus, and earth mingles in the air. Books line the walls. Cups wait quietly on hooks. And at the center of it all is The Authenticitea Barista—less a person, more a presence. They don't just take your order. They *listen*—to the pauses, the sighs, the stories not yet spoken.

A young woman hesitates at the counter, journal in hand.

"I don't know what to order," she says, the weight of uncertainty tucked in her voice.

The Barista studies her, then reaches for hibiscus and ginger, "Something to bring clarity," they say. "Let it steep. The answer will come."

Nearby, an older man sits at the window, tracing the rim of his cup.

Without a word, The Barista sets down a blend of chamomile and honey. A quiet acknowledgment. A silent invitation to exhale.

In the corner, a teenager pulls out their earbuds, curiosity tugging as they unfold a napkin that reads:

No one leaves with all the answers. But something always shifts. Because *A Cup of Authenticitea* isn't meant to solve everything. It's meant to help you remember what matters.

And so, people return.

Not just for the tea.

But for the permission to steep in the questions.

For the stories that rise with the steam.

For the quiet nudge that they, too, are still steeping.

Just like you.

A GUIDE TO THE AUTHENTICITEA TASTING NOTES

– Sip Slowly –

Before you settle into your seat and savor the stories steeped throughout this café, there's something I'd love for you to know.

After each story shared here at *The Authenticitea Café*, you'll find a *Tasting Note,* an invitation to pause and explore the tea featured in that sip, not just with your senses, but with your spirit.

It's an invitation to slow down and notice
the aroma that rises,
the flavor that lingers,
the texture that stays behind.

Each note offers more than description, it offers connection.
To experience the tea as a mirror.
To meet the moment it holds.
To uncover what it stirs within you.

These tasting notes capture the essence of each brew. Its mood, its memory, its message, guide you inward through gentle prompts and mindful reflections. Some guests taste right away, letting the moment steep while it's still warm. Others let the note linger, returning when the time feels right.

There's no one way to engage, just your way.

Because, like tea, reflection invites patience and presence.
So take your time. Return as needed.
Your next *Cup of Authenticitea* is just a page away.

A CUP OF AUTHENTICITEA

A Cup of Discovery

Leaning into curiosity, uncertainty, and wonder

SIP 1: A STEEPED BEGINNING

-Alora-

It felt real. The laughter. Conversation. Sitting on the bed like nothing had changed. And for that breathtaking moment, it hadn't.

Alora stepped into the rain, the echo of that dream still clinging to her. She wasn't planning on leaving the house. But suddenly, still felt impossible.

The downpour blurred the city lights, washing the streets in a muted glow. She pulled her hood tighter over her head, but the effort was futile as droplets still found their way down her face, mixing with the silent tears she had long stopped trying to hold back.

She pushed open the door to *The Authenticitea Café*, a soft bell chiming above her. Warmth wrapped around her like a nicely heated blanket, the scent of roasted beans and spiced chai grounding her just enough to remember how to move forward.

She scanned the room, spotting an empty corner table by the window. The spot her friend would have claimed instantly, insisting they always sit where they could people watch.

Her sister friend.

The ache in her chest intensified, a dull throbbing that made her shoulders tense. Inhaling deeply, she placed her bag on a chair, removed her wet coat, and proceeded to the restroom.

Inside, she braced herself against the sink, staring at her reflection in the dim fluorescent light. Her eyes were red-rimmed, her skin damp from rain and grief alike. She reached for a paper towel, pressing it to her face as if she could wipe away more than just the moisture clinging to her cheeks.

She exhaled shakily.

Last night was a dream, except it was more than that.

She had *seen* her.

She had *talked* to her.

Her friend had been right there, sitting on the bed. They were talking and laughing like nothing had changed. In that impossible, beautiful moment, the world held its breath; time stood still, and everything felt whole again.

Until she woke up and the weight of reality came rushing back.

But something about that dream, about that conversation, had settled inside her, softening the unbearable edge of loss. It didn't erase the pain, but it whispered something she hadn't been able to find on her own.

Her friend was gone. Settled where souls go when this life ends.

Alora felt the ache of that loss, trusting in time she'd be okay too.

She ran another napkin under cool water, pressing it against her face before stepping back into the café.

As she approached her table, she stopped short.

A cup of tea sat waiting for her.

The steam curled up in soft tendrils, filling the air with a light floral scent. Something faintly sweet and grassy, like wildflowers brushing against sunlight. The liquid shimmered pale gold, nearly translucent, as if it held the memory of morning dew.

Beside it, a napkin with delicate scripted words.

Alora paused, then reached for it.

She glanced toward the counter where The Barista stood, watching her with an expression that made her wonder if they somehow knew exactly what she was thinking.

Alora whispered, "thank you", then traced the letters with trembling fingers, her breath catching in her throat.

The world outside was still dark, rain-soaked, and uncertain. But in this moment, with the warmth of tea in her hands and the quiet echo of something greater than understanding, she remembered the first time she felt it.

Loss.

Followed by… presence.

A quiet, undeniable knowing.

For as long as she can remember, grief was woven into her family's stories, their gatherings, their shared remembrances.

When Alora was barely in elementary school, her maternal grandmother passed. She witnessed how it reshaped her mother. Not in loud, dramatic ways, but in the quiet shifts; the pause before answering a question, the faraway look in her eyes when she thought no one was watching.

But there was something else.

Something Alora couldn't quite put her finger on.

At night, in the stillness of her room, she felt it most.

A presence.

It would start as a feeling, an awareness just beyond her understanding, like the gentle weight of an unseen hand resting on her shoulder. Then came the shadow.

Standing in the doorway. Watching. Waiting.

At first, she told herself it was a trick of the light, a figment of her restless mind. But night after night, it returned, moving closer, lingering just long enough for her heart to pound before she squeezed her eyes shut. And when she dared to peek again—

Gone.

She never told anyone. How could she? There were no words to describe the way it felt; *not scary, but not entirely safe, either.* Not threatening, but undeniably *there.*

Then, one night, curiosity overtook fear.

She kept her eyes open. She didn't look away as the shadow moved closer, slow, deliberate. Her breath hitched as it neared, as something in the air shifted, thickened.

Then—

A touch.

Gentle. Fleeting. Familiar.

And just like that, it disappeared.

What should have terrified her instead left her with a strange, quiet comfort. Because in that moment, she *knew.*

She didn't understand it. She couldn't explain it. But she *knew.*

This post death presence begun appearing not long after her grandmother passed, lingering just beyond comprehension. Alora was certain it was her. She recognized the shape, the essence. It felt like her. The shadow never threatened. It watched and waited. As if to remind her, some things aren't meant to be understood. They're simply meant to be felt.

Alora lifted the teacup in front of her, the warmth seeping into her hands.

She had spent so much time doubting, trying to reason with herself, trying to explain away what she had always known to be true.

But last night's dream, reminded her.

She had *seen* her friend. Felt her presence. Shared laughter. Heard her voice.

Just like she had once felt her late grandmother's touch on her shoulder.

She exhaled, bringing the tea to her lips. The warmth spread through her, settling deep.

She didn't need answers. She wasn't meant to have them.

Some things, connections, echoes, whispers from beyond, aren't meant to be explained. They're meant to be felt. And for now, that was enough.

The rain had softened by the time Alora finished her tea, but the world outside still carried the weight of a passing storm. Puddles pooling along the sidewalks, the faint shimmer of streetlights reflecting against wet pavement. She wrapped her hands around the empty cup, as if holding onto its warmth just a little longer.

The napkin with its message lay folded beside her. She unfolded it, tracing the edge of it absentmindedly, letting the words settle into her bones. *Some things are known not by the mind but by the heart.*

She had felt it before. She felt it now.

Taking a breath, she gathered her bag, slipping the napkin into her pocket before standing. As she turned toward the counter, a figure stepped into her path, The Barista.

They met her gaze with an easy steadiness, the kind that made her feel as if she had been expected all along.

"Did you enjoy your tea?" they asked, their voice calm, unhurried.

Alora stood still, her fingers tightening slightly around the strap of her bag. The question felt bigger than it was meant to be.

"It was exactly what I needed," she admitted. Then, after a pause, she added with a hint of wonder— "What was it?"

Their lips curled into a knowing smile. "Silver Needle. A white tea. Gentle, but it lingers."

Alora nodded slowly. "Yes… it does."

The Barista nodded, wiping their hands on a cloth before sliding them into the pockets of their apron. "Good tea has a way of showing up at the right time."

Alora glanced down, unsure of what to say to that. She wasn't even sure why she had come here tonight, only that it had felt like the right place to be.

When she looked back up, The Barista was watching her, not with curiosity, but with the kind of quiet understanding that didn't demand explanation.

"Come back soon," they said, their smile small but certain. "Something tells me you're just getting started."

Alora took a deep breath and gave a small nod before heading for the door, the bell chiming softly as she stepped back into the night.

The air was still damp, but the rain had stopped.

A Taste of Knowing

A quiet moment to feel what's real

—Inspired by Silver Needle Tea—

Mood Pairing: For when you're sensing something you can't explain but know to be true.

Steep Time: Slowly. Let the insight come to you in whispers, not declarations.

Body: Light and lingering. A quiet confidence that stays even after the moment passes.

Origin: Rooted in reflection. Steeped in trust. Best sipped in silence.

Color & Clarity

The brew is barely golden, almost clear, almost invisible.

But presence doesn't need to be bold to be real.

It only needs to be felt.

What quiet truth is revealing itself in your life, even if you can't yet name it?

____

____

____

Aroma

Breathe in. The scent rises like memory: delicate, a touch of hay, something familiar but hard to place.

You don't have to understand it to receive it.

What have you sensed lately that feels meaningful, even if it defies explanation?

____

____

____

Flavor

Take a slow, imagined sip.

The taste is smooth, slightly sweet, and steady. It lingers, not loud, but lasting.

What have you felt that you know is true, even if no one else sees it?

____

____

____

Aftertaste

A calm that follows. A knowing that stays.

What insight or feeling are you taking with you from this sip?

____

____

____

SIP 2: BREWING CURIOSITY

-Autumn-

Autumn had always loved the crisp invitation of fall, how it whispered that change was in the air. The shifting leaves, the cool bite of morning wind, the city humming with movement. It all made the world feel like it was on the cusp of something. But today, instead of feeling awakened by the season, she felt caught in its pause.

She wrapped her coat tighter as she stepped onto the sidewalk, the morning chill pressing against her skin. Around her, the city surged with certainty, horns blaring, heels striking pavement, conversations clipped with purpose. Everyone seemed to know exactly where they were headed.

Except her.

Autumn was suspended in the space between doing and becoming. Between effort and outcome. Between sending and hearing back.

Inside *The Authenticitea Café*, the contrast was immediate. Warmth enveloped her as the scent of jasmine and honey curled in the air. She paused, eyes closed, letting the softness of the space settle around her like a familiar blanket. With a quiet breath, she unwound her scarf and let the door close behind her.

The city moved on. But for Autumn? Life felt still.

Waiting for the email that would tell her if she got the job. Waiting for the results from a recent doctor's visit. Waiting to see if the project she poured her heart into would gain any traction.

She took a seat in the center of the café, her fingers tightening around the strap of her bag as if it could ground her. Her thoughts churned, even as her surroundings soothed.

Then came the Barista, calm, deliberate, placing a small porcelain teacup glazed in soft cream with faint gold veins running through it, like cracks that had been mended with care. A wisp of steam rose, floral and toasty. Barley, perhaps. Chrysanthemum? She couldn't quite name it, but it smelled like something she needed.

With a smile, the Barista slid a napkin next to the cup.

Autumn glanced at it. Simple, hand-written:

Her fingers traced the words, a small sigh slipping from her lips.

"Nice," she murmured, looking up as The Barista lingered at the edge of the table. "But waiting is so hard."

The Barista smiled. "It is," they said after a pause. "We think of waiting as wasted time, as something to endure before we get to the real part of life. But sometimes, it's where the real work happens."

Autumn sighed, wrapping her hands around her cup. "I just wish I knew how things would turn out. It's like… I've done everything I can, and now I'm stuck hoping."

"That's the hardest part," The Barista agreed. "You've planted the seeds, but you don't get to control when they bloom." They tilted their head slightly, watching her. "What would it feel like to trust that what's meant for you is already in the works; even if you can't see it yet?"

Autumn stared down at her tea, letting the steam meet her face as she watched the leaves release their essence into the water.

The Barista's voice was gentle. "This moment isn't about pushing. It's about tending."

Autumn took a sip of her tea letting it linger on her tongue. She had spent so much energy trying to fast-forward through this part, rushing toward answers, convinced that she could only find peace once she had the answers.

But now, wrapped in the café's warmth, something in her began to soften. The in-between, while not ideal, didn't have to be all bad, it could be a pause filled with quiet possibility.

The kind that teaches you how to be more patient, not by holding your breath, but by letting it out.

The Barista was on to something. She could call a friend. Get lost in a favorite book. Pick up a hobby just for fun, not for progress. This didn't have to be wasted time. It was an opening. A hidden space to catch her breath before things picked up again.

As if sensing the shift within her, the Barista gave a small nod before retreating behind the counter.

Autumn sat a little taller, her breath steadier, her hands still wrapped around the cup. She reached for the napkin again, eyes landing on the words neatly written there:

Sometimes, the in-between is the most honest place to be.

She folded it carefully and slipped it into her bag, as if tucking away a truth still forming, but already beginning to matter.

A Taste of the In-Between

A pause between who you are and who you're becoming

—Inspired by Oolong with roasted barley, chrysanthemum, and a touch of honey—

Mood Pairing: For the moments when you're not quite here, not quite there, just somewhere in between.

Steep Time: Let it rest longer than usual. Some flavors need time to surface.

Body: Smooth and layered. Earthy yet floral. Like holding steady in a season of change.

Origin: Born from liminal spaces. Grown in transitions. Best sipped with curiosity.

Color and Clarity

Amber with a soft cloudiness—neither fully clear nor completely opaque.

This is not a moment of definition, but one of unfolding.

What feels a little uncertain, but still really matters to you right now?

____

____

____

Aroma

Warm barley rises first, grounding and familiar. Then comes chrysanthemum—curious, floral, gently awakening. Breathe deep. Notice the tension and tenderness coexisting.

What are you noticing that you hadn't before?

____

____

____

Flavor

The oolong holds steady, anchoring the brew with strength.

Chrysanthemum brings softness. Honey rounds the edges.

Together, they offer a flavor that invites both patience and presence.

Where are you being asked to trust without rushing?

____

____

____

Fill in the blank: I don't have the full answer yet, but I trust that ____________________________________.

Aftertaste

A hint of sweetness lingers—proof that even the uncertain can be beautiful.

What lesson is the in-between offering you today?

____

____

____

Affirmation: I am allowed to be in process. Growth doesn't always come with a plan.

SIP 3:
A STIR FROM WITHIN

-Allison-

In a world that applauds mastery and expects perfection, knowing when to begin again, without a finish line in sight, takes its own kind of courage.

Allison stepped into the cafe, the question trailing her like a loose thread: was she chasing another spark that would fizzle, or was she finally learning to trust the way her energy moved? She had felt this before, that quiet thrill of beginning. A flicker of something new pulling her forward. But she also knew what often followed: the unease that crept in when the glow began to dim.

Her usual seat by the window was open. She slid into it, grateful for the familiar corner where so many of her musings had taken root. The Barista approached, as if already expecting her, and placed a steaming cup in front of her, the scent of citrus and ginger curling into the air.

As to be expected, a folded napkin rested on the saucer. She picked it up.

She wrapped her hands around the teacup. The scent rose, steeping ginger and citrus, bold and sharp, yet comforting. There was a brightness to it too, something unexpected and slightly sweet. Blood orange, maybe?

She brought the cup closer, feeling the warmth press into her palms. The liquid shimmered with a deep amber hue, tinged by a soft red glow from the juice swirled within.

Her first sip was fire and light. Ginger-forward, earthy and awakening. The citrus followed, clean and vibrant. But it was the blood orange that lingered, tart, complex, just sweet enough to surprise her.

Reminding her of the time she first wanted to learn to play the piano.

She hadn't thought about that in a while. How she once believed the piano would be *it*. Her thing. The one passion she'd carry through life like a second language.

She had begged her parents after church one Sunday, inspired by the musician who played with such joy and command. She imagined herself doing the same, filling rooms with music, speaking emotion without words.

But what followed wasn't ease. It was resistance. Frustration. Her fingers stumbled more often than they soared. The music stayed just out of reach. And slowly, that glow faded.

As a child, she had always been drawn to rhythm, to movement. Music made her feel unstoppable, boundless, free. The Sunday choir at church was her first taste of that freedom, where clapping hands and stomping feet created something larger than any one voice could achieve alone. The joy of it filled her chest, made her feel alive.

But it wasn't the singing or the clapping that captured her heart the most, it was the piano. The way the keys danced beneath the hands of the church musician, the way they commanded both melody and emotion, the way they told a story without a single word.

"I want to play the piano," she told her parents, determination shining in her young eyes.

Her parents saved up and purchased her a keyboard. They signed her up for lessons.

Allison took another sip of tea, grounding herself in the present as she thought back to how that journey had unfolded.

Learning the piano was nothing like she had imagined. She practiced when she could. But no matter how much effort she poured in, the notes never flowed the way she imagined. Doubt crept in replacing her excitement and commitment to keep showing up.

Years later, as an adult, she bought a piano hoping to rekindle the spark. A hobby to balance out work. She pictured herself playing effortlessly, filling space with song. But the same struggle returned. The same tension.

And that's when she realized, it wasn't the piano she longed for. It was what she thought it represented.

And it didn't end at the piano. It was calligraphy. A foreign language. Learning about Health and Fitness. All these beautiful beginnings she dove into with full-body enthusiasm, only to feel the pull to move on before she "excelled."

Allison looked down at her tea, now fully steeped, the rich amber color deep and inviting. Was this new adventure calling her for the right reasons? Or was she chasing another illusion of passion?

The Barista returned, cup in hand. "You know," they said with a smile, "I once knew someone who brewed ginger tea at the start of every adventure. Said it reminded them that growth rarely feels comfortable at first, but it always wakes you up to something greater."

Allison looked down at her tea, now fully steeped, the color deepening with each breath. She nodded slowly.

"Like an adventure in a cup," she murmured.

"Exactly," the Barista replied.

She took another sip, letting the warmth settle like an ember, as if it were reminding her of something she was only just beginning to understand.

Passions aren't always meant to be mastered, she realized.

The piano and her other fleeting adventures hadn't been failures. They were mirrors, reflecting who she was in those moments, and what freedom felt like when it first sparked in her chest.

And this new spark?

She didn't have to carry it forever.

She just had to let it carry her for now.

A Taste of Adventure

When courage flickers and you let it catch fire

—Inspired by Citrus Ember: Ginger root, orange peel, lemongrass, and a splash of blood orange juice—

Mood Pairing: For when you need to speak up, show up, or take that first brave step.

Steep Time: Quick and awakening. Just enough to light the spark.

Body: Zesty, punchy, and warm. A blend of brightness with a smoldering kick.

Origin: Brewed in moments of decision. Best sipped with intention and a touch of fire.

Color and Clarity

A rich, sun-kissed hue with a tinge of red-orange glow, like the golden hour before a bold decision. It doesn't just shine, it simmers.

Where in your life do you feel lit from within, not just seen from outside?

____

____

____

Aroma

A sharp zest rises first—ginger and citrus making their presence known. It's bold but not overbearing. Energizing, not overwhelming.

What's trying to get your attention right now? What's calling you to move?

____

____

____

Flavor

A burst of ginger at the front, bright citrus in the middle, and lemongrass softening the finish. This sip doesn't ask you to be fearless—it reminds you that you're already brave.

Meditation prompt: Breathe in through the nose… feel the spark. Exhale slowly… and name what you're ready to do next.

Aftertaste

A warmth that lingers in your chest. A steady ember, not a blaze. Confidence doesn't shout. It glows.

What part of you is ready to rise?

____

____

____

Affirmation: My courage doesn't need permission. It only needs presence.

SIP 4: THE BOLD BLEND OF INDEPENDENCE

-Indie-

Indie wasn't trying to rebel. Not exactly. But there was something about being told who she should be that never quite sat right with her. She had spent most of her life being shaped by tradition, by assumptions, by well-meaning voices that said, *this is who you are* without ever asking.

But lately, that shape didn't fit.

She sat at her usual table in *The Authenticitea Café*, staring past the window's soft reflection. The air hummed quietly as something inside her buzzed, a recent conversation echoing in her chest like a challenge she hadn't agreed to meet.

The Barista approached, their steps unhurried. With a gentle clink, a steaming cup was placed before her. "Peppermint and sage," they said with a knowing smile. "For clarity and strength."

Indie wrapped her hands around the cup. The scent alone was grounding, bright, crisp, and steady. She took a slow sip, letting it settle into her.

It tasted like truth. Like the quiet, steady kind of defiance, the kind that doesn't shout, but simply chooses.

This is who I am. And I get to decide what that means.

She had felt this tension before. It was woven into her childhood, in the subtle and not-so-subtle ways she had been told who she was supposed to be. She was the youngest, and the only girl, in a house full of brothers. From the beginning, the expectations placed on her had been different. Chores were assigned with a future in mind. Hers, apparently, was to learn how to take care of a household, a husband, a family.

"Girl, you need to learn how to cook," her mother had often said, placing a cookbook in front of her. "You should know how to prepare a good meal. One day, your husband will appreciate it."

Indie had never understood why her brothers weren't held to the same standard. If cooking was such an essential skill, shouldn't everyone learn it? She had asked once, only to be met with a sigh and a dismissive wave of the hand. "We're talking about you."

For years, she had pushed back in small ways. She would chop vegetables with reluctance, follow recipes half-heartedly, and find excuses to be anywhere but the kitchen. When her mother scolded her for lacking interest, she had bit her tongue, resisting the urge to say what she truly felt, that she didn't want her worth to be measured by how well she could serve someone else.

It wasn't until she left home that she truly confronted her feelings about cooking. At first, she avoided it entirely, surviving on takeout and quick meals that required no effort. But over time, something shifted. She met people who cooked not out of obligation but out of love; for themselves, for their friends, for the joy of creation.

One evening, a friend invited her over for dinner, handing her a cutting board and a knife.

"Want to help?" she asked casually. There was no pressure, no expectation, just an invitation to be part of something.

As they worked side by side, laughter filling the space between them, Indie felt something loosen inside her. Cooking didn't have to be about fulfilling someone else's needs. It could be about connection, about creativity, about nourishing herself in ways that had nothing to do with duty.

Now, as she lifted her tea once more, she thought about how far she had come.

The independence she had fought for wasn't about rejection; it was about renewal. About deciding what traditions to carry forward in her own way. She would cook, not because she had to, but because it brought her peace. And that, she realized, was power.

A soft smile curved at the corners of her lips as she spotted a folded note tucked beneath her saucer. The Barista's signature touch. Unfolding the slip of paper, she read the handwritten words:

Indie traced the words with her fingers, letting their meaning settle into her. This wasn't just about cooking. It was about the many ways she had felt confined by expectations. Ways she was still learning to unlearn. Her struggle wasn't about rebelling against everything but about discerning what truly mattered to her.

She thought back to the conversation that had unsettled her earlier. The assumption that she should be someone she wasn't, that she should shape herself to fit someone else's version of success. But just like with cooking, she had the choice. She could reclaim the parts that felt right and let go of the rest.

Taking another sip, she felt a quiet sense of resolution settle over her. She didn't have to reject everything; she just had to choose. And she chose herself.

A Taste of Grace

Strength with softness. Power in peace.

— Inspired by Bold Grace: Peppermint & Sage Herbal Infusion—

Mood Pairing: For when you need to stand tall with an open heart and a clear mind.

Steep Time: Let it steep a little longer. This kind of clarity takes its time.

Body: Cool, smooth, and quietly powerful. A refreshing calm with an herbal backbone.

Origin: Rooted in resilience. Grown in humility. Best sipped in moments of self-respect.

Note: Grace is not weakness, it's wisdom.

Color and Clarity

A pale green tint with a silvery shimmer, like morning light on dew-covered leaves. Gentle, but not fragile. Still, but never stagnant.

Where in your life are you being asked to lead with both courage and compassion?

____

____

____

Aroma

The scent is crisp peppermint forward, sage trailing close behind. Cool clarity meets sacred strength. A reminder to inhale the moment fully.

What parts of yourself are asking to be seen without judgment today?

____

____

____

Flavor

The mint wakes you up. The sage grounds you.
Together, they offer a sip that steadies your voice and softens your edges.

Fill in the blank: I am strongest when I _______________ with grace.

Aftertaste

A cool clarity lingers. Not sharp, not sweet. Just clean. Just right.

Grace doesn't always announce itself. It simply arrives and changes the air.

Affirmation: I lead with presence. I walk in grace.

SIP 5: FINDING YOUR FLAVOR

-Aria-

Aria stepped into the sunlight, her curls glinting like a quiet truth finally spoken. A gentle breeze brushed against her scalp, sending a ripple of sensation through her, part confidence, part nostalgia. As she strolled down the street, she caught glimpses of her reflection in passing windows; her hair full, vibrant, unapologetically hers.

Just as she was approaching the door to the café, the familiar chime of the door opening caught her attention. She instinctively stepped aside, making room for the person exiting, until she paused mid-step.

"Wait, Jean?"

The woman in the doorway blinked before breaking into a broad smile. "Aria! Wow, it's been forever!"

Aria laughed, taking in Jean's warm, effortless presence. "It really has! You look amazing."

Jean tilted her head, eyes twinkling. "Right back at you. Those curls are everything."

Aria ran a self-conscious hand through her hair, smiling. "Thanks. It's been a journey but I'm finally learning how to have fun with them."

Jean nodded knowingly. "I love that. –Listen, I'd stay and catch up, but I'm already late heading to an event across the street." She reached for the door handle, holding it open for Aria. "Enjoy your tea. Always a treat."

"Good to see you," Aria called after her, stepping inside.

The moment she crossed the threshold, the scent of steeped spices, hints of citrus, and something soothingly familiar. The Barista, wiping down the counter, glanced up and smiled.

"Good to see you. Your curls are lovely," they said.

Aria smiled, tucking a stray strand behind her ear. "Thanks."

"Beautiful curls," a customer nearby chimed in with a nod.

Aria smiled, fingers instinctively reaching for a curl. "Thank you," she said, though something stirred within her at the words. Compliments, simple and kind, yet it sent her mind spiraling back through the years—through all the versions of herself and her hair that had shaped her journey.

She found a seat near the window, settling in just as The Barista approached. Before she could place an order, they placed a cup of tea in front of her, its color soft and golden, a light steam curling toward her like a whispered memory.

"Velvet Oolong," they said gently, sliding a napkin beside the cup. The edges were slightly crumpled, as if it had been folded and refolded more than once. She picked it up and read…

She traced the words with her fingertips, and just like that, she was a little girl back in the salon chair, the sharp scent of chemicals filling her nose.

The steam rose again, and she brought the cup closer, the scent floral and toasted, familiar, but not quite.

There was something in the flavor that reminded her of her younger self waiting patiently beneath the surface.

The first time she got a relaxer, she thought she was doing what she had to do. Everyone around her had straight hair, it was what was expected, what looked "presentable." But no one warned her about the burning. The way the chemicals would sear into her scalp, leaving angry welts that took days to heal. No one told her that beauty could be painful in a way that made her wonder if it was worth it.

Her mother sighed as she looked at her daughter's irritated scalp, and chunks of hair seeped in between the combs and brushes. "Enough of this," she had said, shaking her head. And just like that, she made a decision.

Chop, chop, chop.

The sound of the scissors echoed in Aria's memory as she stared at her reflection in the salon mirror. The relaxer was gone, but in its place was something else, a new chemically treated style.

"This will help," her mother had assured her, rubbing activator through her freshly cut hair. "No more burns, no more sores."

But it wasn't the solution they had hoped for. Instead of freedom, Aria was left with another kind of burden; dripping curls that required constant maintenance, a scent that lingered long after wash day, and an identity that still didn't feel like her own.

Then came the fire.

It started as a joke. Her brother, laughing as he flicked a lighter near her hair, testing a theory. A quick flick, a burst of heat, and suddenly, flames licked at her curls.

Panic surged through her as she frantically patted at her head, dousing the fire before it could do serious harm. The damage was done, though. Some of her hair was gone, singed beyond repair. Her mother was horrified. Aria was left with more than just lost strands. She was left with the fear of ever trusting another chemical process again.

And yet, years later, she returned to relaxers. It was what she knew, what seemed like the only option. Until the day she finally stopped.

"We thought that was our only choice," a voice murmured.

Aria looked up from her tea and blinked. Across from her sat her younger self. A girl no older than ten, feet swinging just above the floor, fingers idly twisting the ends of her damp curls. Her wide eyes held a question.

Aria sighed, placing her cup down. "We did. For a long time."

Her younger self frowned. "It smelled bad."

Aria let out a small laugh. "It really did."

The girl leaned forward, resting her elbows on the table. "But then we went back to relaxers. Why?"

The truth was heavy, sitting in Aria's chest. "Because we didn't think we had another choice. We thought that was just how it had to be."

"But eventually we learned that sometimes, it takes years before we realize what was true all along."

Her younger self scrunched her nose slightly at the smell of the tea in front of them. "So… what happened?"

Aria exhaled. "We stopped. No more chemicals, no more forcing our hair into something it wasn't."

The girl's fingers played with her curls again. "Were we scared?"

Aria nodded. "We had no idea what our real hair even looked like. But it turned out, it had been there all along, waiting."

The younger girl smiled. "We just had to take care of it."

Aria returned the smile, reaching across the table to tuck a curl behind the girl's ear. "Yeah. Just like we learned healthier ways to take care of our whole self."

A Taste of Ease

A moment to exhale

— Inspired by Velvet Oolong: Orchid, cream, and roasted chestnut —

Mood Pairing: For when you're ready to exhale, release the tension, and simply be.

Steep Time: No rush. Let it unfold slowly, like an unhurried morning.

Body: Silky and smooth, with notes that glide rather than land. Soft curves. Steady warmth.

Origin: Rooted in receptivity. Grown in moments where nothing is forced. Best sipped when you're ready to loosen your grip.

Color and Clarity

A warm golden hue, like afternoon light through soft curtains.
Not brilliant, not bold, just gently present.

What might open if you stopped trying so hard and gave things space?

____

____

____

Aroma

The scent is tender—floral like orchid but rounded by a creamy warmth.

Faint nuttiness lingers, grounding it all in comfort.

What comforts are calling you to pause and savor, even in a busy season?

____

____

____

Flavor

A soft bloom of orchid first, followed by mellow cream and the cozy depth of roasted chestnut.

This isn't a tea that demands—it invites.

Where could more softness invite more truth into your life?

____

____

____

Meditation prompt: Place one hand over your heart.
Breathe into that space.
Ask yourself: Where can I release just a little more?

Aftertaste

Lingering warmth. A gentle reminder that grace doesn't have to be grand—it just has to feel right.

What might shift if you moved with more ease today?

____

____

____

Affirmation: I don't have to force what's meant for me. I move with softness, not struggle.

SIP 6: STEEPING IN FAITH

-Faith-

She was carrying a quiet heaviness today, not a crisis, but a weight that asked to be acknowledged.

Lately, she'd been discovering new layers of herself. A new self-awareness tool was completely shifting how she saw herself, her energy, her patterns, even how she made decisions. It was like she was seeing herself, and others, for the first time. And she wanted more.

Every insight pulled from her birth data felt illuminating, until that quiet voice from her past crept in again, *are you drifting too far?*

Faith stepped into the café, the air warm with the soothing scent of steeping chamomile and honey. This place had always felt sacred; not because of any doctrine, but because it gave her space to exhale. To pause. To listen.

Across the room, Daniel sat at their usual spot, already sipping tea. He looked up and smiled. He'd always been the one she could talk to when spiritual questions felt too heavy to carry alone.

She sat down, her body relaxing into the chair. The Barista returned moments later, setting down a pale porcelain cup filled with golden-hued tea, light steam curling toward her face. A folded napkin sat beside the saucer.

Her eyes lingered on the message. A breath escaped her lips, part relief, part prayer.

She wrapped her hands around the cup. It was warm, faintly floral. A hint of something sweet; vanilla maybe, or honey, rose with the steam. She didn't need to name it. She only needed to hold it.

Daniel tilted his head. "What's the word today?"

She passed him the napkin. He read it, then looked up. "Timely."

"I've been learning so much about myself lately," she said. "Like... deep, internal stuff. Why I do what I do, how I respond to people, how I recharge. It's helping me understand myself in ways I've never had language for. And it's helping me love people better, too."

Daniel leaned in, curious. "That sounds powerful."

"It is," she admitted. "But I keep wondering, am I doing something wrong? Like, am I walking away from my upbringing? From what I was taught to believe?"

He gave her space to think.

"I mean," she continued, "I still believe in God. Stronger than ever, actually. I just… I want to connect differently. Directly. Not out of fear. Not out of rules. Just… presence."

Daniel nodded slowly. "Doesn't sound like walking away to me. Sounds like walking deeper."

Faith hesitated. "That's how it feels. But then I revisit scriptures like Leviticus 19:31— *'Do not turn to mediums or seek out spiritists, for you will be defiled by them.'* And I start wondering if I've crossed a line. If these tools I'm exploring that include horoscopes, birth charts, even self-awareness work, though they're helping me understand myself and others, are somehow wrong in God's eyes."

Daniel didn't flinch. "Do you feel like you're turning away from God?"

She shook her head. "No. If anything, I feel like I'm drawing closer, without the fear. It's not about replacing scripture. It's about seeing myself more clearly. Like when I read, *'Commit to the Lord whatever you do…'* It reminds me that God sees my heart. He's not afraid of my curiosity. He's in it."

"I love that," Daniel said.

"And *'Before I formed you in the womb, I knew you…'* That one always reminds me that we're not discovering something new. God already placed it there. We're just finally seeing it."

She paused, the warmth of her tea grounding her.

"And lately I keep coming back to this verse, *we are God's handiwork.* What if understanding how I move, how I love… what if all of that is part of honoring the design God already created in me?"

Daniel smiled. "That's the kind of clarity religion can't always teach, but God can."

They both sat in the gentle hush of the moment, tea warming their hands and souls.

"I think I'm finally learning that spirituality isn't about choosing between my upbringing and my evolution," she said. "It's about letting God meet me in both."

Daniel tapped his cup. "So how do you stay grounded in that truth?"

Faith took a thoughtful sip, then said, "I've been thinking about three things that help me move through this without losing myself."

"Let's hear them."

"First, *Keep God first.* Not the fear, not the approval of others. Just God."

"Solid," Daniel agreed.

"Second, *Keep it simple.* I don't need to figure it all out at once. I can receive what resonates and leave the rest."

"And third?" he asked.

"*Keep it real.* I don't have to pretend this is easy. It's tender and it's personal. But God knows me. And I don't think any of this is a surprise."

Daniel smiled wide. "That's a whole sermon."

The Barista returned, this time with their own tea in hand, pausing at the edge of the table. "You know," they said thoughtfully, "I once heard someone say spiritual growth is like steeping tea."

Daniel grinned. "Go on."

"They said you can't force it. Even when nothing looks different, something is always unfolding beneath the surface. Trust takes time. The richest parts come from letting the process work on you."

Faith looked at her tea, golden and calm. "So spiritual connection isn't about striving, it's about steeping."

"Exactly," the Barista said. "Let it steep."

Daniel nodded. "Sounds like what you're doing. Not leaving your faith behind. Just letting it grow."

Faith wrapped her hands around her cup, the warmth grounding her. This wasn't rebellion. It was revelation. She wasn't letting go of God, she was letting go of the fear that she had to meet God a certain way.

Their relationship wasn't about rehearsed rituals. It was about honesty, intention, and trust. And in that sacred stillness, she knew— She wasn't lost.

She was finally listening.

She lifted her tea, whispered quietly, *thank you,* and took a slow sip.

A Taste of Faith

Grounding trust that faith requires

— Inspired by: Rooibos, turmeric, holy basil (Tulsi), and a hint of clove or honey —

Mood Pairing: For when you're walking by trust, not sight. When answers are quiet, but presence is strong.

Steep Time: Let it brew slowly. Faith is never rushed, it's revealed.

Body: Rich, golden, and grounding. A warm embrace for the uncertain heart.

Origin: Born in surrender. Rooted in reverence. Best sipped in moments of quiet belief.

Color and Clarity

Golden amber, like sunlight in a still room.

Not meant to dazzle, meant to warm.

Where in your life are you being asked to trust without proof?

____

____

____

Aroma

Earthy turmeric rises first, softened by sweet rooibos and holy basil.

A subtle spice hums beneath it, like a whisper from something ancient.

What moments in your life have felt guided, even if you couldn't explain why?

____

____

____

Flavor

Deep and mellow with subtle warmth.

Tulsi and clove hint at something sacred. Rooibos offers comfort.

This sip doesn't demand—it invites you to believe.

What belief are you holding onto—even if it feels fragile?

____

____

____

Fill in the blank: *Faith, for me, feels like* ________________________.

Aftertaste

Lingering calm. A warmth that doesn't fade quickly—like a promise kept.

What would change if you trusted that you're already held?

____

____

____

Affirmation: I trust the unfolding. Even in silence, I am guided.

SIP 7: THE SPICE OF UNCERTAINTY

-Coach Roberts-

What if the bravest thing you ever did didn't start with confidence, but with curiosity?

Coach Roberts stepped into the tea shop, the hum of conversation blending with the melody as the soft strumming of a guitar wove through the air. She immediately recognized it as an old tune, the kind that played on late-night drives, where the road stretched wide with possibilities and curiosity whispered, *What if?*

The scent of ginger and lemongrass curled around her, bold and invigorating. It struck her instantly—the same scent that had once clung to the edges of a leap she hadn't felt ready for, but had taken anyway. Back then, she hadn't known where it would lead. But she'd shown up. She always did.

The café held its usual charm, worn tables gathered in pockets of quiet reflection and lively conversation. Near the window, golden sunlight spilled across a group of young adults, their animated voices bouncing between sips of tea. A round table in the center swayed with laughter, the kind that didn't hold back.

Then—

"Coach Roberts? No way!"

She turned at the familiar voice, her gaze landing on a table filled with faces she hadn't seen in years, former players, mentees, dreamers she had once guided.

"Look at you all!" she said, shaking her head with a laugh. "How is it possible you're grown already?"

"You used to tell us time flies when you're chasing something meaningful," one of them grinned.

Before she could respond, The Barista appeared with a steaming cup, setting it in front of her with that knowing, quiet presence. A neatly folded napkin sat beside it.

Coach Roberts chuckled, already anticipating the wisdom inside. She unfolded the napkin.

She exhaled, letting the memory surface.

"Do you ever think about the time you coached us hard heads?" one of them asked, eyes glinting with mischief.

She smirked, taking a slow sip. The flavor hit smooth, then sparked at the back of her throat; ginger, cinnamon, maybe a bit of orange peel. A blend that didn't ask for permission before making itself known.

"Oh, I can't forget. I still don't know how I got roped into that."

They laughed, but beneath their amusement was something unspoken, an understanding.

Boldness had never been about having all the answers. It had been about stepping up despite uncertainty.

She hadn't been a basketball coach. She hadn't even played the sport competitively. But when no one else had volunteered, she had stepped in, watching game footage late at night, scribbling plays in notebooks, learning just enough to help them believe in themselves.

"You led us to an undefeated season," Jordan said, shaking his head. "And you barely knew the difference between a pick and roll and a fast break when we started."

"True," she admitted, setting her cup down. "But I did know how to believe in you. And that made all the difference."

They nodded, the weight of the statement settling between them.

"Well, whatever you did," one of them said, leaning back with a grin, "it worked. We still talk about that season like it was yesterday."

"Yeah," another added, raising their cup in her direction. "Here's to taking chances on things you don't think you're ready for."

Coach Roberts let out a breath of laughter and clinked her cup against theirs. "Here's to all of us figuring it out as we go."

The conversation shifted, rolling into new stories, updates on careers, cities they had moved to, lessons learned since high school. Eventually, one by one, they drifted out, their goodbyes punctuated with promises to stay in touch.

As the last of them left, Coach Roberts sat back.

The Barista placed a fresh pot of tea on the table, the steam curling into the air between them.

"You ever notice how ginger sneaks up on you?" they said, pouring another round. "Starts smooth, then—bam—the heat kicks in."

Coach Roberts smirked, taking a sip. "Like an unexpected full-court press."

The Barista chuckled. "Exactly. Some people avoid that kind of heat. Others learn to lean into it."

She let the words settle. She had spent a lifetime stepping into challenges, trusting that she'd figure things out as she went. But had she grown too careful? Too measured?

She glanced down again at the napkin. *Bravery isn't about knowing the outcome—it's about showing up anyway.*

The Barista tilted their head. "So, what's next, Coach?"

She wrapped her hands around the warmth of her cup. "Guess it depends on whether I'm still willing to play the game."

She looked around the tea shop, at the empty chairs where her former players had sat, at the space they had once filled with stories of uncertainty, possibility, and belief. They had taken their leaps.

Had she stopped taking hers?

She took another sip, the warmth spreading through her, the spice lingering on her tongue.

Some cups were meant to be poured with a little extra spice.

And maybe, for her, it was time for another sip.

A Taste of Brave Momentum

The moment when courage catches up to movement

— Inspired by The Ginger Snapback: Ginger root, cinnamon, orange peel, and a hint of clove —

Mood Pairing: For when you've waited long enough, and it's time to leap, speak, or shift.

Steep Time: Not too long. This blend wants to move. Steep it just long enough to ignite.

Body: Bold, spicy, and energizing. A snap of heat balanced by citrus zest.

Origin: Brewed in the belly of brave decisions. Best sipped on the edge of what's next.

Color and Clarity

Amber with fiery edges. A visual reminder that momentum glows from the inside out.

Where in your life are you gaining the courage to move, even if imperfectly?

____

____

____

Aroma

Spice-forward. Ginger rises first, then cinnamon and clove bring the heat. Orange peel slices through like sunlight between doubts.

What's reigniting your fire, even if it once felt burned out?

____

____

____

Flavor

A bold zing. Ginger speaks loudest, but the cinnamon holds it steady.
Clove deepens the brew while orange keeps it bright.
It's a snapback, not to what was, but to who you've always been.

What are you reclaiming right now, momentum, voice, purpose?

____

____

____

Fill in the blank: *I may have paused, but now I'm ready to* __________.

Aftertaste

A tingling warmth that stays long after the sip is gone.
Momentum doesn't have to roar. Sometimes, it hums.

What's your next brave move, even if it's small?

____

____

____

Affirmation: I am in motion. Every step is a return to my power.

SIP 8: A STRONG INFUSION

-Briana-

Some people search for answers in books, in stars, in other people's opinions. Briana searched in steam.

She hesitated at the door of the tea shop, fingers tightening around the strap of her bag. The scent of steeping leaves wrapped around her, hints of vanilla and cinnamon curling through the air. Usually, the aroma was enough to ground her, to remind her why she came. But today, the familiar comfort barely touched the knot twisting in her chest.

She had always come here in search of clarity. But today, clarity felt as elusive as the steam rising from a fresh cup, close enough to see, yet always drifting just out of reach.

Opening the door wider, she stepped inside. The warmth of the space embraced her, the quiet murmur of conversation blending with the gentle clinking of porcelain. Soft light filtered through shelves lined with glass jars, each filled with delicate leaves and fragrant spices, waiting for their moment to bloom. It was a place that usually made her feel steady. But today, her mind was a storm.

The thought had been following her for weeks, whispering in the quiet moments, steeping in the back of her mind. An opportunity. A chance to step into something new, something uncertain. And yet, every time she leaned in, the fears swirled stronger.

What if I fail?

What if I embarrass myself?

What if no one understands why I'm even trying?

She let out a breath as she sank into her usual seat. A few moments later, The Barista appeared with a steaming cup, placing it before her with their signature touch, a folded napkin resting on the saucer.

Briana smirked despite herself. This ritual had become as familiar as the doubts in her mind.

She traced the edge of the napkin before unfolding it, her eyes skimming over the handwritten words.

She inhaled sharply, as if the words had caught her off guard. She had spent so much time avoiding the question that she had never let herself answer it. Did she care enough to risk failing? To risk being seen trying?

She wrapped her hands around the cup, letting the warmth seep into her fingers. A soft swirl of vanilla mingled with the boldness of spice. something grounding but quietly fiery, like the kind of strength that didn't shout but simmered beneath the surface. The scent reminded her of warmth earned after a long storm.

She closed her eyes for a moment. There was a steadiness in it. A quiet courage. A strong infusion that didn't chase the fear away but made room for it to breathe.

Growing up, Briana had learned early on that some dreams made sense to people, and some didn't. She had always been the one with a cup overflowing with curiosity, sampling new interests like an ever-changing blend. One day, she imagined herself a journalist: the next, a bookstore owner. A scientist. A counselor. A traveler. Each possibility steeped in excitement, until she was reminded that she it was best if she choose just one.

She spent years trying to do just that. Picking paths. Changing course. Wondering if she was lost when, in reality, she had simply been searching.

Now, the search had led her here, to a moment where a new adventure called to her. But instead of excitement, she felt paralyzed.

What if people didn't understand? What if they thought she was just chasing another fleeting interest? What if she tried…and failed?

She exhaled, watching the steam curl from her cup. Purpose, she realized, might be less like a plan and more like this tea; bold, soft, surprising. It didn't demand clarity right away. It just asked for her presence. To steep long enough to reveal something new.

The Barista returned, settling into the chair across from her. They stirred their tea absentmindedly, watching her over the rim of their cup.

"You look like someone caught between staying or leaping into something new."

Briana let out a breathless laugh. "That obvious?"

They nodded toward her untouched napkin. "You read the message?"

She ran her fingertip over the ink. "Yeah."

"And?"

Briana sighed. "I don't know. I'm afraid. Of looking foolish. Of making the wrong choice. Of failing."

The Barista tilted their head. "Why does failure feel like the worst thing that could happen?"

Briana opened her mouth, then closed it. No one had ever asked her that before.

"I guess because...it's embarrassing," she admitted. "People will see. They'll know I tried and didn't make it."

The Barista tapped their spoon against the rim of their cup. "So, you'd rather not try at all?"

Briana winced. The words hit like a splash of scalding water. "I want to try. I just don't know how to silence the doubt."

The Barista smiled softly. "You don't have to. Doubt doesn't mean don't, it just means you're stepping into something new. And that's where purpose often lives."

Briana sat with that. What if it wasn't about erasing fear, but about steeping in it? Letting it be part of the process, knowing that the strongest flavors often come from the leaves that sit in hot water the longest.

She lifted her cup, the warmth curling through her palms. Maybe it was time to take the first sip of this new adventure—uncertainty, fear, and all.

A Taste of Strength and Shivers

The quiet strength that remains

— Inspired by Steady Ember: Spiced Vanilla Chai with Rooibos —

Mood Pairing: For when you're steady on the outside, but the inside's still catching up, or vice versa.

Steep Time: Long and patient. This one needs time to deepen and settle.

Body: Bold, creamy, and warm with a little heat beneath. Equal parts comfort and courage.

Origin: Rooted in resilience. Best sipped when you're holding it together, even if you're still shaking.

Color and Clarity

Dark amber with hints of deep rust and gold.

Not sharp. Not soft. Just sure.

Where are you holding steady, even while something inside is shifting?

____

____

____

Aroma

Vanilla soothes first. Then the spices arrive: chai, clove, a touch of cinnamon.

It smells like warmth earned, not borrowed.

What scent or memory reminds you of your own resilience?

____

____

____

Flavor

Creamy vanilla wraps around bold spice.

The rooibos roots the blend, while the chai adds complexity.

It's not trying to dazzle, it's here to endure.

What inner ember is still glowing, even after the storm passed?

____

____

____

Fill in the blank: Even when I shake, I am still ________.

Aftertaste

A soft heat that stays low and steady.

It doesn't ask for applause, just space to keep burning.

What would it feel like to be proud of your quiet strength?

____

____

____

Affirmation: I am not fragile for feeling. I am powerful for continuing.

A Gentle Stir: Between Discovery & Alignment

From curiosity to clarity, every sip of discovery stirs something new within us. As we lean into alignment, what once felt uncertain begins to settle, revealing what truly fits.

A Cup of Alignment

Leaning into defining moments

SIP 9: BLENDING EVERY CHAPTER

-Jean-

Jean sat at *The Authenticitea Café*, staring out the window at the glow of an entrance she was scheduled to walk through any moment now. The warm amber light spilled onto the sidewalk, illuminating the confident strides of guests entering the event.

Inside the café, the scent of chai and bergamot curled through the air, mingling with the soft hum of conversation. The chatter of passersby spilled out each time the doors opened, but she remained still, fingers tightening around her bag.

Networking events had always been a challenge. Not because she disliked people, quite the opposite. She loved learning about others, hearing their stories, finding those unexpected points of connection. But introductions? That was a different story.

How did one neatly package a life filled with twists, turns, and ever-evolving passions into a single, digestible answer?

Her phone buzzed. A message from a friend: Are you coming?

She exhaled, rolling her shoulders back, trying to shake the weight of expectation. Taking a deep breath, she asked herself, "Was she going?"

Her eyes drifted downward to the small piece of paper tucked underneath her fresh cup of tea. She hadn't noticed it until now. Curiosity sparked as she unfolded it, tracing the delicate, slanted handwriting.

Her breath caught slightly. Who had left it there? Was it meant for her, or had she simply discovered it at the perfect moment? She glanced around the café, scanning the faces of other patrons, but no one seemed to be watching her.

The tea's aroma drifted upward; soft, floral, grounded. Lavender, perhaps. Rooibos. Something slightly sweet. She brought the cup to her lips and took a slow sip. It was unexpected, layered in a way that made her pause, close her eyes, and taste again.

Through the quiet, the Barista's voice rose gently from behind the counter. "That one's called *More Than One Note,*" they said, making eye contact with Jean. "It doesn't need to be defined by a single flavor."

Jean rested the cup against her chest, feeling the warmth settle into her ribs.

Jean had spent years navigating introductions like an ever-changing script, adjusting based on her audience. In professional settings, she gave the practical version: sharing what she did at her day job. But in other spaces, she hesitated. Was she a teacher? A realtor? A coach? A consultant? A creative?

The question *What do you do?* always felt like a test she couldn't answer correctly.

Sometimes, she answered too vaguely, and people appeared unimpressed. Other times, she over-explained, watching their polite nods as their attention drifted elsewhere. Each time, she wondered—why did it feel so difficult to claim her full self?

She had met people who answered with confidence and clarity, but their paths were linear, their titles straightforward. Jean envied their simplicity, yet she knew she wasn't built that way. Her identity was a composition, not a single note.

The Barista now standing across from her, holding a cup of tea. "Are you okay, you seem deep in thought."

Jean smiled, wrapping her hands around the warmth of the cup. "Just thinking about how hard introductions can be."

The Barista nodded, stirring their tea thoughtfully. "You know, self-expression is a lot like brewing tea. Some people like a single, strong flavor. Others prefer a blend."

Jean tilted her head. "A blend. I like that."

"Some of the best teas don't fit into one category," The Barista continued. "They're floral and herbal, sweet and earthy. They don't need to be defined by one note, they just need to be enjoyed for what they are."

Jean chuckled softly, shaking her head. "So I should just introduce myself as a tea blend?"

The Barista grinned. "Why not? Instead of trying to explain every ingredient, just invite people to take a sip. Here, let's practice. How would you introduce yourself if you weren't worried about impressing anyone?"

Jean hesitated, then exhaled. "I explore different paths, blending my love for learning, teaching, and creating. I don't fit into one box, and honestly, I like it that way."

The Barista lifted their cup in approval. "That's it. No need to justify or explain, just let people experience who you are."

Jean sat with the words, letting them steep in her mind like a perfectly brewed tea. Maybe introductions weren't about fitting into a mold but offering others a taste of what made her unique.

As she left the café and stepped into the event, the weight of needing to fit into a single answer started to lift. The buzz of conversation swirled around her, but instead of hesitation, she felt something different, lightness. The note still rested in her pocket, a quiet reminder.

She knew her story, and she was ready to share it—fully, authentically, and unapologetically.

A Taste of wholeness

Embracing your full layered self

— Inspired by More Than One Note
Lavender, Rooibos, Peppermint, and Rose Petals —

Mood Pairing: For the moments you're learning to hold all of you: the soft, the strong, the still becoming.

Steep Time: Let it steep without rushing. Complexity takes time to bloom.

Body: Delicate yet grounded. Soft petals, strong roots. Like a garden growing inward.

Origin: Composed from many layers. Best sipped when you're reconnecting with all that makes you, you.

Color and Clarity

A soft blush or muted gold with shifting hues. It looks different from every angle.

Like you, never just one thing. Always becoming.

What parts of yourself have you overlooked that are asking to be seen again?

___

___

___

Aroma

The scent moves in waves, floral notes meet fresh herbs, grounded by something deeper. A breath of balance.

What contrasts within you are actually complements?

____

____

____

Flavor

There's no single taste that dominates. Lavender, mint, Rooibos, maybe something woody beneath. It asks you to slow down, not to figure it out, but to receive it.

Where have you grown more whole, not in spite of your layers, but because of them?

____

____

____

*Fill in the blank: I am not just this or that—I am*____________________.

Aftertaste

Gentle complexity. The feeling of having met yourself more fully. Not a resolution, but a reunion.

What would it feel like to be at peace with all that you are?

____

____

____

Affirmation: I am not a contradiction. I am a composition.

SIP 10: THE NEXT POUR

-Brittany-

The café door swung open, releasing a swirl of roasted coffee and spiced tea into the crisp evening air. Brittany stepped inside, her Air Max 95s landing with an easy rhythm against the worn wooden floor. She moved with an effortless kind of confidence. Not the kind that asked for attention, but the kind that made people look twice anyway.

She was used to being noticed. Not for speaking the loudest or taking up the most space, but because she carried something, a presence, a quiet magnetism. Her style spoke before she did: bold prints, unexpected layers, colors that clashed just enough to work. She had a way of making streetwear feel like poetry.

But tonight wasn't about being seen. Tonight, she needed space to think.

She slid into the first seat she saw, adjusting the sleeves of her Adidas hoodie, fingers absentmindedly tracing the embroidered details. Fashion had always been more than fabric to her, it was language. A way to communicate without ever opening her mouth.

Lately, though, a question had been gnawing at her.

Who am I beyond what I wear? What parts of my story have I yet to step into?

A soft clink pulled her from her thoughts. A ceramic cup, placed quietly on her table. No order necessary. That was the thing about this café, it had a way of seeing people.

Next to the cup, a slice of lemon placed neatly on the saucer. Next to the saucer, a scripted napkin, waiting.

Brittany smirked. She knew this game.

She picked up the napkin.

She let out a slow exhale, her eyes drifting toward the tea in front of her.

It was striking; an electric, inky indigo that seemed to shimmer as it swirled. Butterfly pea flower tea. She recognized it instantly. A tea that transformed with just a drop of lemon, shifting from deep blue to a bold, regal purple.

She picked up the cup, letting the warmth settle into her palms. If she squeezed in citrus, the tea would change just like that. A reflection of adaptation. Of leaning into what's next.

She took a sip, the taste grounding and floral, laced with something almost unspoken.

Her mind drifted back, red Filas in third grade, the Air Maxes she chased in high school, the thrifted jacket that once made her feel invincible. Every piece she had ever worn had been a chapter. A version of herself, stitched into fabric, walking through time.

She set the cup down, tapping her finger on the napkin, thoughtful.

Maybe self-expression wasn't just about what she put on. Maybe it was also about what she allowed herself to become.

Beyond the sneakers.

Beyond the prints.

Beyond the labels.

"Deep in thought tonight?"

The voice was familiar, warm, steady. Brittany glanced up to see Aaron standing nearby, a knowing grin, easy, familiar.

She hadn't seen him since the accident. And now, here he was, upright, steady, moving with that same easy confidence. Relief settled in her chest.

"Didn't expect to see you here," she said.

Aaron lifted his own cup, tapping the rim lightly. "I was just on my way out. Saw you come in and figured I'd stop by and say hi."

"I'm glad you're okay," she said simply.

He gave a small nod, rolling his shoulder as if testing it. "Me too." His gaze flickered to the tea in front of her. "What about you? What have you been up to?"

She smirked, folding the napkin between her fingers. "You ever feel like you're changing, but you don't know into what yet?"

Considering her words, Aaron pulled out a chair and set his cup down.

"All the time," he said, leaning back. "Growth sneaks up on you. One day, you're wearing something because it's the most comfortable piece of clothing you got, and the next, it just… doesn't fit the same way anymore."

She nodded, tracing the rim of her cup. "I used to think my style said everything about me. But now, I'm wondering if I've been hiding behind it instead."

Aaron leaned forward on the table wrapping his hands around his cup. "Maybe it's not hiding. Maybe it's translating. You've always used fashion to tell a story, right? Maybe now, you're just ready to tell it differently."

She let that sink in.

It was true, she had spent years curating her identity through fabric and texture, layering parts of herself in patterns and movement. But there were pieces of her that had nothing to do with what she wore. Stories she had yet to tell.

She thought about the first time she fell in love with a pair of sneakers; the red Filas, the way they made her feel like she could run faster, jump higher. The first time she felt seen in an outfit, the way it transformed her confidence.

But there were other moments too. The time she gave away her favorite jacket to someone who needed it more. The nights she sat in silence, no layers, no bold colors, just herself and the weight of her thoughts.

Style wasn't just about what you put on. It was about what you let go of, too.

She looked at Aaron, a slow smile forming. "You ever tried this tea before?"

He shook his head.

She picked up the lemon wedge from the saucer, squeezing it into the cup, watching as the deep blue shifted into a vibrant purple.

"Watch this," she said, nudging the cup toward him. "It changes. Just like that."

Aaron watched the transformation, nodding. "Clever."

She smirked. "Yeah. It really is."

She tucked the napkin into her pocket, letting its weight settle, a quiet reminder, a nudge forward.

Whatever came next, she wasn't just wearing the story she was living it.

A Taste of Becoming

Celebrating change

— Inspired by Butterfly Pea Flower, Lemongrass, Mint & Citrus —

Mood Pairing: For when you're in the middle of blooming, not finished, not fixed, just beautifully unfolding.

Steep Time: Let it steep as long as needed, the color and clarity evolve with time.

Body: Light, bright, and refreshing. Floral with a cool spark and citrus lift. A sip of becoming in motion.

Origin: Crafted for transitions. Best sipped when you're embracing the now, even as you grow toward what's next.

Color and Clarity

Starts a deep indigo, then shifts when citrus is added: violet, periwinkle, even pinkish hues.

This tea doesn't hide its changes. It lives them.

Where in your life are you mid-transformation, and can you name the beauty in that?

Aroma

Fresh and light, with lemongrass lifting the blend and mint giving it movement.

A whisper of change in the air.

What scents or signs remind you you're growing, even if it's subtle?

____

____

____

Flavor

Cool and citrusy, with a floral undertone that surprises you.

Not too strong, not too soft—just evolving with each sip.

Where are you allowing yourself to be in progress, not perfection?

____

____

____

Fill in the blank: I am learning to become without needing to ________.

Aftertaste

A clean finish with just a hint of mint and lemon.

It leaves you awake, alive, and open to more.

What truth about yourself feels clearer now than it once did?

____

____

____

Affirmation: I am becoming. I don't need to rush what's already unfolding.

SIP 11: AN UNFILTERED BREW

—Charlotte and Sterling—

What do you do when the dream you built doesn't feel like yours anymore?

Charlotte traced the edge of her table, her gaze distant as the late morning light spilled across the tea shop window. The silence hung between them, not awkward, just full of everything they hadn't said yet.

Sterling leaned back in his chair, fingers drumming once against his knee before stilling.

"It's a big decision," he said finally, the words landing softly, but with weight.

Charlotte didn't turn. "I know." Her voice barely carried. She paused, then added, "It just feels like… if we let it go, we're letting go of everything we said we wanted."

Their house had once held so much hope. The open floor plan, the oversized backyard, the quiet promise in each extra room. They pictured dinner parties echoing through the walls, holidays threaded with laughter, a revolving door of family and friends.

But life hadn't unfolded in those rooms the way they imagined. Most remained untouched.

Mornings were quietly lived in the sunlit kitchen nook. Evenings found them curled up in the den, speaking softly if at all. The dining room sat mostly untouched. The guest rooms stayed ready, for guests who never came.

Had they built a home, or just an idea of one?

The Barista approached, placing two cups down gently in front of them. A quiet nod. A folded napkin, slipped between the saucers like a note passed in class.

The scent rose first, warm vanilla and toasted coconut folded into oolong's earthy base, subtle but impossible to ignore. Sterling wrapped his hands around the cup, grounding himself in the comfort it offered.

Charlotte picked up the napkin and unfolded it, reading aloud:

She exhaled softly, tapping her fingers against the table. *Why did this feel familiar?*

And then it hit her.

"Funny," she said, leaning back. "This reminds me of our wedding."

Sterling smirked. "You mean the wedding that almost wasn't ours?"

She nodded, stirring her tea. "I remember how hard that was. We didn't want to disappoint anyone."

They had followed the script, a grand venue, a designer gown, a guest list filled with distant relatives and friends of family they barely knew. Each decision, made with good intentions, pulled them further from themselves.

It wasn't until Charlotte stood in a boutique, staring at her reflection in an intricate, beaded gown, that the reality settled in. The dress was breathtaking, but it didn't feel like *her.*

The entire wedding didn't feel like *them.*

That night, they sat on the kitchen floor, takeout between them, staring at contracts, invoices, and a growing list of things that felt more like obligations than choices.

"I keep telling myself it'll feel right once the day comes," Charlotte admitted, pushing a piece of paper aside. "But the more we add, the less I see *us* in it."

Sterling set down his fork. "So, what do we do?"

Charlotte hesitated, the truth catching in her throat. "What if we let it go?"

The words felt impossible.

And freeing.

Sterling studied her for a moment, then nodded. "Then we let it go."

So, they started over.

Gone was the ballroom, replaced by a sunset ceremony in a small garden with only their closest loved ones. The towering cake? Swapped for a homemade pie from Charlotte's grandmother's recipe. The dress? A soft, pale blue pantsuit, simple, elegant, completely her.

Their vows, written by hand, spoken with full hearts, were not for an audience but for each other.

"It was one of the hardest decisions we made," Charlotte said, bringing her cup to her lips. "But once we did, it was the easiest thing in the world."

Sterling nodded, glancing down at the napkin again. "And now here we are, different decision, same feeling."

The Barista, wiping a table nearby turned to them. "You know, authenticity is like tea. It changes as it steeps, but its essence never wavers."

Sterling raised a brow. "Meaning?"

"Tradition and expectation can blend together, but the richness comes from what *you* bring to it. The key is honoring both without losing yourself."

Charlotte let the words settle. Home wasn't about square footage, it was about intention.

She turned to Sterling, a sense of clarity washing over her. "We thought we needed the big wedding to prove something. Turns out, all we needed was what felt right." She let out a breath. "Maybe the house isn't so different."

Sterling's gaze softened. "I guess it's not about *losing* something. It's about making space for what actually fits."

She nodded, the weight lifting. "So maybe it's time we stop holding onto the house we thought we needed, and start choosing the home that feels like *us*."

Sterling lifted his cup in a small toast. "To vows we make to ourselves."

Charlotte tapped cup against his. "And living them every day."

A Taste of Self-Honoring

Courageously choosing yourself without apology

— Inspired by Whispered Oolong: Toasted Coconut & Vanilla Bean—

Mood Pairing: For when you're ready to honor what you feel, want, and need, even if no one else understands it.

Steep Time: Let it steep slowly. Self-honoring isn't rushed, it's revealed.

Body: Smooth and warm with a subtle sweetness. Gentle on the surface, steady underneath.

Origin: Rooted in quiet clarity. Best sipped when you're choosing yourself, softly and surely.

Color and Clarity

Golden with a warm amber glow, like candlelight reflecting off still water.

Not bold, not faint, just sure of itself.

What's quietly true for you, even if you haven't said it aloud yet?

____

____

____

Aroma

A gentle blend of toasted coconut and vanilla, resting atop the floral whisper of oolong.

It smells like the kind of comfort that comes from alignment, not approval.

What parts of your life feel most like "you" right now?

____

____

____

Flavor

Vanilla softens the sip, coconut adds depth, and oolong carries it all with ease.

There's nothing urgent here, only resonance.

Where are you learning to honor your needs without guilt?

____

____

____

Fill in the blank: Honoring myself means allowing ________.

Aftertaste

A quiet richness that lingers longer than expected.

Like a truth you finally allowed yourself to say, and now can't unfeel.

What would it look like to fully choose yourself today?

____

____

____

Affirmation: I don't need permission to honor what's true for me.

SIP 12: A BOLD CUP OF COURAGE

-Matthew-

Matthew stepped into the café, his shoulders carrying the weight of a decision he wasn't sure he was ready to make. The air inside was warm, scented with spices and citrus. He let out a slow breath as his eyes scanned the cozy space, the shelves lined with books and teacups.

At the bar, The Barista was already steeping something, their movements calm, intentional. Without asking, they slid a deep amber-hued cup of chai with a hint of orange zest and vanilla toward him. The steam curled around his face, wrapping him in its warmth.

Next to the cup sat a neatly folded napkin, the words scrawled in familiar ink:

Matthew swallowed, his fingers resting on the edge of the napkin as he read it again. The timing, almost eerie. He hadn't said a word about why he came in, about what was on his mind. And yet, here was a cup of bold, spiced chai, the kind that wakes the senses, stirs something deep, and lingers long after the last sip.

He lifted the cup, breathing in the aroma, cardamom and cinnamon swirling with citrus, grounding yet invigorating. The first sip was fire, a heat that settled in his chest like something awakening. It didn't ask for permission. It just was.

He glanced up at The Barista, raising an eyebrow. "How did you know?"

The Barista simply smiled, wiping down the counter with an easy rhythm. "People don't usually come in with that look unless they're standing at some kind of edge."

Matthew huffed a quiet laugh, shaking his head. "That obvious, huh?"

"Not obvious," The Barista said, pausing for a moment. "Just familiar."

Familiar. The word stuck with him. He let his gaze drift toward the window, where the sky had begun its slow shift toward dusk, golden light spilling into the café. His attention caught on a bookshelf near the corner, its contents a mix of novels, poetry collections, and travel guides. One title stood out, *Beacons of the Coast - A Guide to the Lighthouses That Have Stood the Test of Time.*

Lighthouses. His mother had loved them. She used to say they were proof that even the smallest light could guide the way. They had spent countless afternoons driving to the coast, climbing the spiraling staircases, standing at the top where the wind howled, looking out at the endless stretch of water. She always told him that courage wasn't just about braving the storm, it was about trusting that a light, however distant, would lead him through.

One of his dear old friends had been the one to remind him of that. Years later, after she was gone, a friend, he recently reconnected with had sent him a note, scrawled in handwriting that was recognizable and foreign after so many years apart.

"You were always the one searching for the light, Matthew. Maybe it's time to be the one who follows it."

But then there was his father. The voice of logic, of stability. Just last week, his father had called to check in. "Proud of you, son. You're steady, reliable. Not like those people who chase dreams and end up lost." The words had been spoken with love, but they had landed heavy, pressing against Matthew's chest like an anchor. He had nodded along, even as something inside him recoiled. Was stability really the only measure of a life well lived?

For years, he had followed the practical path, the one that made sense to others. A stable career, a clear trajectory, a respectable routine. But deep down, a quiet voice had been nudging him toward something else, something that felt more like him.

And now, here he was, at a crossroads.

The hesitation wasn't just about fear of change. It was about legacy, expectations, and the quiet pressure of being someone others relied on.

Growing up, stability had always been the goal. His parents worked hard to ensure he had opportunities, security, the kind of life where 'what ifs' didn't come at the cost of survival. So, choosing something uncertain felt almost... selfish.

And yet, wasn't there also a responsibility to honor what called to him? To not just exist within a life that felt safe, but to build one that felt true.

His fingers tightened around the warm ceramic. His heartbeat quickened, just slightly. The weight of logic told him to stay put, but for the first time in years, the quiet voice of longing was louder.

He let his gaze wander back to the book. *Beacons of the Coast*. His mother had always told him lighthouses weren't just for ships lost at sea, they were for those who needed a moment to pause, to realign, to remember where they were going. Maybe he had spent too long looking for the perfect course when all he needed was a light to remind him he wasn't lost, just in between destinations.

Another sip, and he let the heat of the chai settle deep. He wasn't sure he had all the answers, but courage wasn't about certainty. It was just about deciding to begin. He folded the napkin, slipped it into his pocket, and for the first time in a long time, allowed himself to consider, really consider, a life that fit.

A Taste of Courage

When it's time to begin again

— Inspired by Spiced Chai with Orange Zest & Vanilla—

Mood Pairing: For when the next step feels shaky, but you're taking it anyway.

Steep Time: Give it time to bloom fully. Boldness is best brewed with presence, not pressure.

Body: Warm, spiced, and layered. Strong enough to wake something up, smooth enough to keep you steady.

Origin: Born at the edge of uncertainty. Best sipped when you're stepping into the unknown, with heart wide open.

Color and Clarity

Rich amber with golden edges, like sunlight breaking through storm clouds.

It's the color of movement after pause.

Where are you being called to move forward, even if you're not "ready"?

____

____

____

Aroma

Spice hits first, clove, cinnamon, and chai warmth, followed by a soft wave of vanilla and a lift of citrus.

It smells like confidence cracking open.

What does courage feel like in your body right now: tight, expansive, trembling, alive?

____

____

____

Flavor

Zesty orange opens the sip. Spice holds the center. Vanilla offers comfort as it all settles.

This tea reminds you: you can be bold and tender at once.

What are you walking toward, even with a racing heart?

____

____

____

Fill in the blank: My next step may be small, but it's a step toward

____.

Aftertaste

Lingering warmth, like a promise kept to yourself.

A quiet *yes* to what's next.

Affirmation: I honor each forward step. I am braver than my hesitation.

SIP 13: TRUSTING THE STEEP

-Sarah-

Sarah hadn't planned to stop here. In fact, she hadn't planned to go anywhere in particular. She was just walking, wandering through town, weaving in and out of small businesses, trying to escape the anxious thoughts pressing against her chest.

Graduation was just weeks away, and everyone around her seemed excited. Her classmates talked about college, jobs, moving away. Words that made her stomach twist into knots. Was she ready for this? Had high school even prepared her?

For the past four years, her world had been carefully structured. Teachers who understood her, parents who protected her, routines that kept things from feeling overwhelming. She had an Individualized Education Plan (IEP) since she was in middle school, something that helped create a structure that worked for her, that made the chaos of school just a little more manageable. But there was no IEP for life, she thought. No carefully crafted plan to help her navigate adulthood, to make sure she didn't get lost in the noise. Soon, that safety net would disappear. She'd have to navigate everything herself. Would people accept her? Would they see her quirks as something to admire, or just something to tolerate?

She always felt different. Not in a way that made her special, just... separate. Like she was existing on a slightly different frequency than everyone else. Socially, she never quite fit in. Small talk exhausted her, and she second-guessed everything she said in conversations, worried she'd sound strange. Fashion never felt intuitive either, her clothes were comfortable, practical, but never seemed to match the effortless confidence of her classmates. She wasn't the kind of person who could just *be* in a space without feeling the weight of being watched, analyzed, or misread.

The Authenticitea Café wasn't even on her radar until she found herself standing outside, staring at its softly lit windows. Something about the space felt inviting, like it wouldn't demand anything from her.

She stepped inside.

Sarah kept her head down as she approached the counter, pretending to study the menu while her heart thudded in her ears. The Barista, who had been drying a cup, glanced at her and smiled.

"First time here?"

Sarah nodded.

Without asking what she wanted, The Barista set the cloth aside and reached for a tall glass, filling it with ice before pouring a liquid so pale and golden it almost looked like sunlight caught in water. The scent of lavender and citrus lifted into the air, mingling with the café's warmth.

"Lavender Lemon Spark," they said, sliding it toward her. "We don't usually make it, but sometimes, the right thing isn't on the menu."

Sarah hesitated before wrapping her fingers around the chilled glass. The first sip was unexpected, cool and soothing, but with a hint of something bright and surprising. She didn't realize how tense she had been until the taste melted into her, softening the tightness in her chest.

The Barista set down a small napkin beside the drink, the edges neatly folded.

Handwritten across it was a single sentence:

Something inside her softened.

She had spent so much time worrying about where she belonged, if people would like her, if she'd make the right choices. But what if belonging wasn't about molding herself to fit?

What if her place in the world had already been carved out, waiting for her to step into it?

She took another sip of the tea, its coolness settling deep in her chest.

Sarah had always been the quiet one, the one who preferred the edges of a room to its center.

Her teachers described her as "insightful," "creative," "a deep thinker." She liked that. But she also knew those were just nice ways of saying she wasn't the loudest, most confident, or the one who raised her hand first.

Social anxiety had followed her like a shadow for as long as she could remember. Simple things, speaking in class, introducing herself, even ordering food at a restaurant, had always required extra effort.

Now, the safety nets were disappearing.

There wouldn't be a teacher stepping in when she looked overwhelmed. No school counselor checking in to see how she was adjusting. No familiar routines cushioning the impact of big changes.

She worried that once high school was over, her quirks, her quietness, her need for space, her love of books over parties, would make her feel even more out of place.

She was excited for what was next. But also terrified.

As she took another sip, The Barista leaned against the counter, watching her thoughtfully. "You're graduating soon, right?"

Sarah blinked in surprise. "Yeah... how did you know?"

The Barista smiled. "You've got that look, kind of like you're carrying the whole world on your shoulders." They gestured toward the window. "I remember that feeling. Graduation is supposed to be exciting, but it's also terrifying."

Sarah hesitated before asking, "Did you know what you wanted to do? When you graduated?"

The Barista let out a short laugh. "Not even close. I thought I was supposed to have a plan, so I picked something that sounded responsible. Went to college, switched majors three times, took a job I thought I'd love… but it took me a while to realize that figuring things out doesn't happen on a schedule."

Sarah traced a finger along the condensation on her glass. "So, you didn't have it all figured out either."

"Nope," The Barista said, shaking their head. "And honestly? I think that's normal. There's no single right way to enter adulthood. Sometimes, you have to try things that don't fit before you find what does."

Sarah considered that. It wasn't the kind of answer she was used to hearing. Most adults seemed to expect her to have it all figured out. But this… this felt more real.

Sarah sat at a small table by the window, hands slightly grasping the glass, watching the world outside move in fast, hurried steps.

She wasn't sure what was next. But she had stepped into this café. She had taken a sip of tea. She had allowed herself a moment to exist just as she was, without forcing herself to be anything else.

A Taste of Patience

Trust timing

— Inspired by Lavender Lemon Spark: Iced Herbal Infusion—

Mood Pairing: For when you're in the middle of waiting, but choosing not to rush.

Steep Time: Cool and extended. Like lessons that only reveal themselves when you're not looking.

Body: Bright, floral, and refreshing. A delicate sparkle balanced by grounded stillness.

Origin: Drawn from patience. Best sipped when you're learning to trust your own timing.

Color and Clarity

Soft violet kissed with gold. Clear, but not loud.

It invites you to slow down and pay attention.

Where in your life are you being asked to trust what's quietly working behind the scenes?

____

____

____

Aroma

Lavender rises first, floral, grounding. Lemon lifts it, bright and awakening.

Together, they offer calm momentum.

What scent or sensation helps you return to trust when doubt tries to settle in?

____

____

____

Flavor

Crisp lemon dances first. Then lavender wraps around it, soothing and subtle.

The cold brew gives it clarity, no rush, no heat, just intention.

Where in your life are you learning to honor the process—not just the outcome?

____

____

____

Fill in the blank: Trusting the steep means letting go of ____________.

Aftertaste

A cooling calm with a bright finish.

The kind of clarity that comes after surrender—not control.

What part of your life feels like it's steeping right now?

____

____

____

Affirmation: I release the rush. I trust what's unfolding in its own time.

SIP 14: STILL BREWING

-Zack-

The gym buzzed with energy, sneakers squeaking against polished floors, the rhythmic bounce of the ball echoing off the walls. Zack stood near the doors, watching as his son high-fived his teammates after a hard-fought game.

"Good game, Dad?" his son asked, his eyes bright with adrenaline.

"Great game," Zack said, ruffling his hair. "You had some solid plays out there."

His son grinned before running off toward the locker room with his teammates. "I'll see you later on, okay. Your mom is going to drive you home" He yelled after his son.

"Okay, dad–sounds good," his son said before entering the locker room.

Zack lingered for a moment, hands in his pockets, watching the scoreboard fade to black.

Walking out into the crisp evening air, he exhaled deeply. His son had talent, real talent. Watching him play had stirred something inside him, something he hadn't let himself feel in a long time.

Pride, yes. But also… longing.

He had once been the kid on the field; the one people talked about. The kid with the golden arm, the future pro. The one who could thread a pass through the tightest defense but struggled when the playbook was written in a language his mind couldn't grasp as easily as his hands could grip a ball.

The echoes of the stadium still lived somewhere deep in his memory, the roar of the crowd, the weight of the ball in his hands, the crisp snap of a perfect throw.

But that life had faded like a dream upon waking, replaced by the steady rhythm of fatherhood. A role he embraced, a life he built with pride. And yet, in rare quiet moments like this, he wondered if he had left too much of himself behind while making sure his kids had everything they needed to shine.

He started the car but hesitated before pulling out of the parking lot. He wasn't quite ready to go home.

That's when he noticed a glow. A café sign that read—*The Authenticitea Café.*

He had driven past it a hundred times before, never thinking twice. But tonight, something pulled him in.

The door to the café swung open, letting in the cool evening air as Zack stepped inside. The rich aroma of steeping herbs and honey filled his senses, grounding him in the moment. He found a seat near the window, rubbing his hands together as he exhaled.

Before he could fully settle into his thoughts, a blur of movement outside caught his attention. A man walking past the café suddenly stopped short, did a double take, then turned on his heel and burst through the door.

"No way—Zack Mason?"

Zack blinked as the familiar face came into focus. Jared Thompson. His old high school teammate.

"Jared?" Zack smirked, shaking his head as he stood to clasp hands with him. "Man, it's been years."

"Tell me about it," Jared laughed. "I was just walking by, saw you through the window, and had to make sure my eyes weren't playin' tricks on me." He glanced around. "You a regular here or just happened to stumble in?"

Zack chuckled. "First time. Kind of got drawn in."

Jared pulled out a chair without asking and sat down. "Guess that makes two of us. You still throwin' spirals somewhere, or what?"

Zack smirked, shaking his head. "Nah, those days are behind me. Life took me in a different direction."

Jared nodded, giving a quick little swipe of his finger around the room. "And that direction led you to a mysterious tea shop?"

Before Zack could answer, *The Barista* approached, setting a steaming cup in front of him along with a folded napkin.

"Peppermint and ginseng," they said with a knowing smile. "For clarity and endurance."

Zack smirked. "Sounds like something I could use." He glanced at Jared, then picked up the napkin.

Jared raised an eyebrow. "Wait—you got a note?"

"Yeah, I heard it's something special they do here," Zack smirked.

Unfolding the napkin slowly he quietly read.

He exhaled, staring at the words a little longer than necessary. More. He had never really thought about what 'more' could mean for him.

Jared watched him for a moment. "That hit a nerve?"

Zack leaned back in his chair, rubbing a hand over his jaw. "Man, I don't even know. I've spent so long making sure my kids have every opportunity, I never stopped to think if I still had some of my own left to claim."

Jared nodded. "I get that. I spent years wrapped up in work, making sure everyone else was good. Then one day, I realized I hadn't thought about what *I* wanted in a long time." He shrugged. "Had to figure it out. You should, too."

Zack traced the rim of his cup, feeling the warmth seep into his fingers. "I just don't know where to start."

Jared tapped the napkin. "Maybe that's the point. You don't need to have it all figured out right now."

Zack lifted the cup to his lips, letting the steam curl around his face before taking a slow sip. Sharp, grounding, steadying. Exactly what he needed.

Jared stood, stretching. "Well, man, I gotta go. But first, I think I'm gonna stop by this counter and grab a beverage on my way out."

Zack nodded, still absorbed in his thoughts as Jared made his way to the counter.

He barely registered the low exchange of voices as Jared greeted The Barista. A moment later, they handed him a to-go cup, and, just like with Zack, a folded napkin.

Jared paused, looking down at the note in his hand. His smile faded slightly as he unfolded it, reading whatever words were written inside. He stared at it for a beat, then let out a quiet chuckle, shaking his head.

With a final glance back toward Zack, he tucked the note into his pocket, lifted his cup in a small farewell, and headed for the door.

Zack watched him go, a lingering curiosity forming in his mind, but he didn't ask. Instead, he looked back at his own napkin.

He didn't need all the answers tonight.

Just the willingness to sit with the questions, and see where they might lead.

A Taste of Timeless Growth

Acknowledging growth when you can't see it happening

— Inspired by Peppermint & Ginseng: Herbal Reviver —

Mood Pairing: For when you're somewhere between burnout and breakthrough, and simply choosing to keep going.

Steep Time: Quick and energizing, but don't rush it, clarity comes with intention.

Body: Cool and focused. Crisp peppermint with an energizing undercurrent of ginseng.

Origin: Brewed in perseverance. Best sipped when you're not quite "there," but no longer where you were.

Color and Clarity

A pale golden green, clear, bright, and slightly minty.

You can see right through it, yet still feel the strength beneath.

What are you working through right now, even if it's not fully defined yet?

____

____

____

Aroma

Sharp peppermint clears the fog. Ginseng hums underneath with quiet stamina.

It smells like forward motion, even on tired days.

What's keeping you upright when motivation fades? What's keeping you connected to purpose?

____

____

____

Flavor

Clean and energizing. Peppermint awakens the senses, ginseng brings depth and staying power.

This isn't just a wake-up, it's a stay-with-it.

Where in your life are you honoring progress over perfection?

____

____

____

Fill in the blank: *I may not be done yet, but I'm still* _____________.

Aftertaste

A lingering coolness with a quiet kick of energy.

It doesn't shout. It steadies.

What's reminding you that your process is still valid—even if incomplete?

____

____

____

Affirmation: I am still becoming. And that's more than enough.

SIP 15: THE ART OF BALANCE

-Meghan-

The door to *The Authenticitea Café* swung open, ushering in a crisp autumn breeze. The scent of cinnamon, clove, and honey drifted through the air, weaving through the rich aroma of steeping tea. Normally, Meghan would have savored it, the warmth of autumn wrapped in a single inhale, but today, her stomach clenched.

She hesitated at the threshold, pressing a hand lightly against her belly. Would this be the day the smells overwhelmed her? She hadn't been able to stomach different scents for months, and even her favorite herbal blends had turned on her some days. But she had come anyway. She always came here when she needed a moment of clarity, a gentle nudge, a reason to believe she could find balance again.

Stepping inside, she adjusted the scarf draped loosely around her shoulders and exhaled slowly, testing the air. A hint of vanilla from nearby drink tempered the spices, softening the intensity. So far, so good.

Conversations hummed around her, a comforting white noise, but she still felt the weight of eyes drifting her way. Pregnancy had a way of making an entrance before words were exchanged. She'd gotten used to it, the way strangers marveled at the fullness of her belly, the inevitable questions: *When are you due? Twins? Oh, you must be exhausted!*

She'd smile, nod, answer gracefully. But today, she just wanted to sit. To breathe. To quiet the buzzing thoughts in her mind.

Her business was thriving. Her family was growing. And yet, beneath the excitement was a current of anxiety, an unspoken worry about how she would manage it all. She had one child already, a lively three-year-old who filled her days with laughter and love, but also the undeniable exhaustion of motherhood. Soon, she'd have three. Three tiny humans needing her love, her patience, her guidance. And she still wanted to be *her*—not just *Mom*, but Meghan, a woman with ambitions, dreams, and a business she had poured her soul into building.

She found a corner table, one tucked just enough out of the way but still within reach of the café's warmth. Settling in, she rested both hands on her belly as if negotiating with the universe for reassurance.

Moments later, The Barista approached, placing a steaming cup in front of her without a word. Meghan didn't need to look up to know what would come next. A neatly folded napkin slid across the table. She smiled faintly as she traced the edges before unfolding it.

She let out a breath, her fingers pressing gently over the words. No surprise, just the steady, familiar wisdom she had come here seeking.

"Chamomile and rooibos," The Barista said from where they stood. "For grounding and endurance."

Meghan chuckled softly, tilting her head up to meet their knowing gaze. "Endurance is exactly what I need."

The Barista gave a slight nod, hands resting lightly on their apron. "Open to sharing what's on your mind?"

Meghan hesitated, her fingers curling around the warm cup, the scent wafting up to meet her. This blend, at least, didn't turn her stomach. It smelled…safe. Comforting. "I'm excited," she admitted. "But I'm also terrified. I don't want to disappear into motherhood. I love my kids, I want to be a great mother. But I also want to keep building what I've started, to still be seen as *me*."

The Barista didn't offer quick reassurances, just stood there, letting her words breathe before finally speaking. "Becoming a mother again doesn't erase who you were before. It adds to her."

Meghan ran a hand absentmindedly over her belly, allowing the truth of that to settle in. "But what if I can't do it all? What if I stretch myself too thin?"

The Barista's expression softened. "Then you allow yourself grace," they said simply. "Pace yourself. Some seasons require slowing down, not stopping. You're not losing yourself. You're growing into a version of you that has more to offer, not just to your children, but to yourself."

She exhaled, feeling the tension release from her shoulders. The taste of the chamomile and rooibos lingered on her tongue, warm and soothing, as if reminding her that balance wasn't something to be achieved in one grand moment, it was something found, one sip at a time.

A Taste of Expansion

Holding peace and purpose at the same time.

— Inspired by Chamomile Rooibos Bloom: Herbal Infusion —

Mood Pairing: For when you're juggling many roles, many feelings, and searching for your center.

Steep Time: Let it steep slowly. Balance can't be rushed. It needs space to unfold.

Body: Warm, soothing, and gently grounding. Chamomile softens. Rooibos roots.

Origin: Brewed between motion and stillness. Best sipped when you're seeking alignment, not control.

Color and Clarity

Amber-gold with soft edges. Not perfectly clear, but calm, settled.

It reflects what's real: not flawless, but flowing.

Where are you learning to stay steady without burning out?

____

____

____

Aroma

Chamomile leads with its mellow floral note. Rooibos hums underneath, warm and rich.

Together, they create a scent that slows your breath.

What brings you back to yourself when everything feels off-kilter?

____

____

____

Flavor

Smooth and comforting. Sweet without sugar.

It doesn't pull you in one direction—it gathers you whole.

What are you allowing yourself to release, so you can regain your rhythm?

____

____

____

Fill in the blank: Balance, for me, feels like ______________________.

Aftertaste

A subtle calm, like a breath fully exhaled.

Not a pause. A peaceful continuation.

What would it look like to honor both effort and ease in your day today?

____

____

____

Affirmation: I carry peace within motion. I trust myself to find balance again and again.

Savor the Moment: Between Alignment & Connection

From self-understanding to shared moments. As we pour into connections, our truth flows freely, shaping the bonds we nurture.

A Cup of Connection

Leaning into shared moments, relationships, and belonging

SIP 16: THE COMFORT OF HOMEBREWED MEMORIES

-Hayleigh-

What do you call a place that remembers you, even when you no longer recognize yourself in it?

The question echoed softly as Hayleigh stepped into the café, her suitcase rolling behind her in a gentle rhythm. The wheels hummed against the worn wooden floors, a subtle reminder that she was always in motion. She had just landed back in town for a short visit, just long enough to check in, to remind herself where she came from, before moving on again.

This café was one of her favorite places to visit when she came home. Yet each time she returned, it felt a little different. Or could it be because *she* was different. Life had carried her far beyond the small town where she grew up, into cities and landscapes that once existed only in her daydreams. And yet, here she was, standing in a café she had been coming to since she was a child, taking a moment to breathe before heading home to see her parents.

Home.

The word didn't feel as anchored as it once had. For so long, home had been a fixed point, a place tied to childhood memories and the rhythms of a life she had outgrown. But now? Now, home felt like something she carried with her, something that shifted and stretched with every new place she visited.

The Barista, a familiar face, met her with a warm smile, wordlessly placing a steaming cup of tea in front of her. Resting against the rim was a small, folded napkin—part of a quiet ritual she had come to expect, yet one that never lost its meaning.

Hayleigh returned the smile, a silent exchange of recognition passing between them. She picked up the note, unfolding it carefully, letting the words settle into her.

It was this type of on-time message that felt like home. Her gaze drifted to the tea before her, its deep amber hue swirling with delicate steam.

Oolong.

Neither fully black nor fully green, but somewhere in between, a tea that transformed with each steep, adapting to the water, the temperature, the time. She traced a fingertip along the edge of the cup, absorbing its warmth, the message lingering in her mind.

Fitting.

She wrapped her hands around the cup, letting the warmth seep into her palms.

The world had been calling her for a while now, whispering in unfamiliar landscapes, in new routines, in the spaces where she allowed herself to embrace uncertainty. She had packed up her life, lightened her load, and set out not just to see the world, but to feel it.

But being here, in this café, she couldn't ignore the quiet tug of nostalgia. She thought of her parents' house, the one she grew up in, the creaky stairs, the kitchen that always smelled like pancakes on Sunday mornings, the way the porch light was always left on, waiting for her return. She thought of the family gatherings, the familiar voices, the predictable stories that were told and retold, grounding her in something steady.

She loved them. She missed them.

But she had changed.

This place, this town, it still held echoes of who she used to be, but it no longer defined her. And that was okay. She was learning that home wasn't about geography. It was about connection. It was in the people she met, the stories she collected, the way she chose to move through life.

Taking a slow sip of her tea, she reached for her journal.

There was always something worth documenting.

And today, home was found in this pause, in this sip, in this moment of reflection before stepping back into the life that had shaped her, and the one she was still shaping for herself.

A Taste of Belonging

For remembering what grounds you

— Inspired by Transitional Oolong: Semi-oxidized, smooth and toasty —

Mood Pairing: For when you're craving comfort, not escape. A return to what still holds you.

Steep Time: Let it steep long and slow. Like stories passed down, the flavor deepens with time.

Body: Toasty, rounded, and nostalgic. A warmth that comes from within, not just the cup.

Origin: Rooted in memory. Best sipped when you're remembering, reconnecting, or simply sitting with what once was.

Color and Clarity

A soft amber with coppery glints. The kind of color that feels like fall, like old wood floors and familiar light.

What memory brings you comfort, not because it keeps you stuck, but because it reminds you of your strength?

____

____

____

Aroma

Toasty and warm. Slightly sweet, with a faint hint of stone fruit or grain. It smells like a story you've told a hundred times—but still smile when you do.

What scent always takes you back—and what does it remind you to carry forward?

____

____

____

Flavor

Smooth and mellow, with gentle complexity.
Not bold, but persistent. A tea that doesn't need to prove anything—it just *is.*

What parts of your past are asking to be honored rather than edited?

____

____

____

Fill in the blank: My memories aren't holding me back—they're helping me

____.

Aftertaste

A quiet fullness. Like sitting back after a favorite meal. Like knowing you've kept the best parts with you.

What traditions, people, or rituals still warm you from the inside out?

____

____

____

Affirmation: I am made of moments worth remembering. I carry them with grace, and grow from them with love.

SIP 17: THE PAUSE BETWEEN SIPS

-Serena-

Serena didn't want to be alone. She wanted to share space, not words.

It wasn't isolation she craved, it was invisibility. To exist among others without demand, without question. To breathe without apology.

But the weight of the world still pressed against Serena's shoulders.

It wasn't just one thing, it never was. It was the accumulation of expectations, unspoken thoughts, and assumptions expressed by others. It was the tangled web of emotions, threading through her mind, pulling her in different directions.

She recognized the signs. The need to pull back, to retreat. To step into silence before the noise became too overwhelming.

One place came to mind—*The Authenticitea Cafe*.

It wasn't about socializing. That's what she loved most about it. There, she could sit among others, surrounded by the soft clinking of porcelain and the gentle hum of life moving around her, while remaining in her own space, unbothered, unhurried.

Packing a few things, she made her way to the café. A few traffic stops later, she was sliding into her usual seat, grateful it was still open.

After asking for chamomile with honey, she pulled out her headphones, softening the world around her. The warmth of the cup rested between her hands as she took slow sips, letting the steady energy of the café surround her without demanding anything in return.

Peace.

Her fingers traced the rim of her teacup. The steam curled toward her face, its scent wrapping around her like a familiar embrace. She exhaled slowly. How long had she been doing this, retreating from within?

The memory surfaced before she could stop it, as vivid as if it had happened yesterday.

She had been a little girl, standing in the driveway, eager and hopeful.

"Daddy, can I come?"

Her father didn't look up as he secured the last strap in the truck bed. "Not this time," he said. "Go inside with your mom."

Her brothers smirked, their laughter sharp against her ears. "Stay with the girls. This is boys' time."

Her stomach tightened. The rejection stung more than the crisp morning air.

She clenched her fists. She stomped her feet. She threw a tantrum right there in the driveway, her frustration spilling onto the pavement in angry kicks.

After briefly pulling off, the truck returned.

Her father stepped out, his face unreadable. He didn't scold. He didn't yell. He simply got out of the truck and called her inside the house.

She hesitated, her little heart still pounding with protest. But she went.

The Executioner was waiting.

A lightly stained wooden paddle with a handle, a relic from another time, its surface worn with the names of her brothers and cousins, etched reminders of past warnings. She had never been on the receiving end of it.

Until now.

A few taps. Just two or three. Barely enough to sting.

But that wasn't what hurt.

It was the fact that he had never done it before. That this was the moment he had chosen. That this was how he had responded to her wanting to be included.

The tantrum stopped. So did her words.

For two weeks, she barely spoke to him. First, out of defiance, but then out of something deeper. A peace she didn't yet have the words to name.

In that silence, she discovered something new. At first, it was just the absence of words. Then, it became a space. A place where she could sit with her emotions, turn them over in her mind, let them settle without pressure to explain or be understood. A quiet place that was hers alone.

It was the first time she learned that silence wasn't just absence, it was power.

The soft clatter of a saucer brought her back to the present.

The Barista refilled her cup and placed a folded napkin beside it. A silent offering.

She unfolded it.

Her fingers lingered over the words. She let them settle, much like the quiet that had shaped her over the years.

She didn't need to respond. Not everything required an answer.

Instead, she wrapped her hands around the warmth of her freshly filled cup, feeling its steady presence.

The world around her moved, soft chatter, the faint hiss of the kettle, the occasional scrape of a chair, but she remained still. Observing. Absorbing.

She closed her eyes for a moment, listening.

Not to the noise, but to the space between it.

This was why she came here.

Not for conversation. Not for distraction.

For this.

For the pause. For the breath between thoughts.

For the knowing that she didn't have to fill the silence, she only had to sit with it.

A Taste of Stillness

Honoring silence and inner reflection

— Inspired by Chamomile with Honey —

Mood Pairing: For when the world is loud and your spirit needs soft. A breath between everything.

Steep Time: Let it linger longer than you think you need. This kind of calm isn't in a rush.

Body: Gentle, smooth, and warm. A comfort steeped in surrender, not escape.

Origin: Rooted in restoration. Best sipped in silence, with no expectation.

Color and Clarity

Soft golden glow. Like candlelight or a slow afternoon sunbeam. Nothing flashy—just fully present.

What part of your life is asking for stillness instead of answers?

____

____

____

Aroma

Sweet chamomile with a floral hush, rounded by warm honey. The scent alone slows your heart rate.

What does your version of 'enough for today' smell, sound, or feel like?

____

____

____

Flavor

Warm and mellow with a hint of sweetness.

Each sip says: You don't have to *do* to be worthy.

Where in your life are you ready to take a pause, even if just for a moment?

____

____

____

Fill in the blank: When I pause, I remember _______.

Aftertaste

A calm that wraps around you.

Like being tucked into something familiar and forgiving.

What could rest teach you—if you let it?

____

____

____

Affirmation: I am worthy of rest. I honor the power of pause.

SIP 18: STEEPING INTO CONNECTION

-Addison and Tracy-

Addison stepped into *The Authenticitea Café*, brushing away a stray strand of hair as a soft breeze followed her inside. The scent of the steeping tea wisped through the air. She scanned the cozy space for one person who always knew what to say.

And there she was, Tracy, sitting at their usual table, flipping through a book with a contented smile.

The café had become their meeting place, an unspoken ritual they had stumbled into months ago. What started as casual exchanges over the tea counter had blossomed into a friendship neither of them expected.

"Addison, darling, you look like you've been running a marathon," Tracy teased, tapping her fingers rhythmically on the table before pushing her reading glasses up her nose. "Late night?"

"More like an early morning," Addison groaned, sliding into the seat across from her. She exhaled sharply, running a hand through her hair before resting her chin in her palm. "Work deadlines, life… you know, the usual existential thirty-something crisis."

Tracy chuckled, her laugh rich and full. "Ah, yes. I remember those. Back when I thought I had to figure everything out by forty. Turns out, life keeps surprising you well beyond that."

Before Addison could respond, The Barista appeared, setting down two steaming cups of tea, their scents swirling together, one earthy and grounding, the other floral and bright. A tea napkin rested between them; a single sentence scrawled in careful script:

Addison turned the napkin over in her hands, her eyes flicking to Tracy, who raised an eyebrow knowingly.

"Alright, which one of us is being called out today?" Addison smirked, taking a sip of her tea, a robust oolong infused with hints of lavender and honey. The warmth spread through her, comforting yet awakening, much like their conversations.

If someone had told Addison a year ago that one of her closest friends would be a sixty-five year-old woman who collected first edition novels and unapologetically wore sequins on weekdays, she wouldn't have believed it.

Likewise, Tracy never imagined she'd find such joy in swapping stories with a thirty-something - year-old navigating career choices, dating disasters, and dreams she was still learning how to claim.

And yet, here they were, meeting monthly at this café, their conversations weaving through past and present, wisdom exchanged in both directions.

Tracy loved Addison's energy, her drive, the way she questioned everything and refused to settle. Addison admired Tracy's unshaken confidence, the way she carried a lifetime of stories with both grace and humor.

Despite their generational gap, they found common ground in the way they showed up for each other, as mirrors, guides, and sometimes just a reminder that neither of them was alone.

"I used to think getting older meant having all the answers," Addison admitted, stirring her tea absently. She let the words hang between them, her fingers tightening slightly around her cup. "But the more I live, the more I realize… I have no idea what I'm doing."

Tracy traced the rim of her teacup with one finger, staring into the steam as if lost in the past. A small, knowing smile played at the corner of her lips before she finally spoke. "Welcome to the club, dear. You know what they don't tell you? Even in your sixties, retired and all, you're still figuring things out. The difference is, you stop worrying so much about whether you're doing it right."

Addison sighed, shifting in her chair, the tension in her shoulders slowly unwinding. "That must be nice."

"It is," Tracy said, taking a slow sip of her tea, delicate and rejuvenating.

"But you don't have to wait thirty years to get there."

Addison tilted her head. "How do you mean?"

"Hustle less. Live more. The best stories come from the moments you let yourself be present."

Addison watched the steam curl from her cup, the weight of expectations she had placed on herself feeling just a little lighter. She glanced back at Tracy and grinned. "See? This is why I keep you around," she said.

Tracy playfully smirked. "Darling, I thought I was keeping you around."

They clinked their cups together in an unspoken toast—to friendship. And as their cups met, Addison thought of the words on the napkin. Maybe friendship wasn't just a bridge, it was the road itself, the steady path they walked together, no matter their starting points.

A Taste of Community

Building and bridging friendships

— Inspired by Robust Oolong with Lavender & Honey —

Mood Pairing: For when you're ready to meet someone in the middle—with grace, curiosity, and an open heart.

Steep Time: Medium to long. Let it steep until the strength softens into warmth.

Body: Full-bodied with gentle floral threads. Steady, grounding, and unexpectedly tender.

Origin: Brewed in conversation. Best sipped during honest exchanges and quiet companionships.

Color and Clarity

Deep amber touched with violet undertones, layers of depth that shift depending on the light.

What relationship in your life is inviting you to be more present, more open, or more whole?

____

____

____

Aroma

The strength of oolong anchors it, while lavender rises like breath.

Honey settles in softly, like words said at the right time.

What does connection smell like to you? Grounding? Floral? Familiar? New?

Flavor

Bold and smooth. Oolong takes the lead, but lavender brings balance and honey lingers with warmth.

This is a tea that reminds you: both strength and softness have their place in closeness.

Where are you learning to offer both honesty and grace in your relationships?

Fill in the blank: I am learning that true connection requires _______.

Aftertaste

Lingering complexity. A layered calm.

It doesn't fade, it evolves, just like meaningful relationships.

What bridges have you built lately—or which ones are waiting to be crossed?

Affirmation: I show up fully and listen deeply. Connection begins with presence.

SIP 19: POURING YOUR TRUTH

-Joy-

Some stories don't begin with bold declarations. They begin with silence, with waiting, with the quiet courage to return.

Joy sat in a corner booth at the *café*, fingers wrapped around a ceramic cup. This café had been her quiet refuge for years, a place where she had come to wrestle with uncertainty, to stare at blank pages, and, eventually, to fill them.

She had first walked through these doors when she was caught between exhaustion and ambition. Torn between the weight of her story and the fear of telling it. At the time, she hadn't known if she was ready to write, let alone share, what had been held inside her for so long. But this place kept calling her back, nudging her forward.

This wasn't her first visit.

This place had been calling her back for years. At first, she thought it was the quiet refuge it provided—the kind of space where time didn't rush, where tea steeped slowly, and where the air carried a warmth that hugged her like an old friend. But it was more than that. The café spoke to her.

The first time she had come here, restless and uncertain, she found a note tucked beneath her cup.

She had held onto those words for days, turning them over in her mind, but she hadn't yet picked up the pen.

On another visit, when she sat staring at a blank page, a different note arrived:

She wrote a single sentence that day. Then closed the notebook and left.

Each time she returned, the café greeted her with something new, a quote scribbled on a napkin, a book left open to a passage that felt like a message, a Barista who seemed to know when to simply place a cup of tea in front of her and walk away. The signs were always gentle, never forceful. Invitations, not demands.

Still, she hesitated.

Could she truly lay herself bare on the page? Would anyone care? Would she be seen?

The first time she had asked herself those questions, she had left the café without writing a single word. The second time, she managed a sentence. Slowly, over weeks and months, she filled the pages—sometimes in a rush, other times in hesitant, half-finished thoughts. Some days, she wanted to abandon it altogether.

But she always came back.

And then, one day, after months of stops and starts, she arrived to find another note waiting for her beneath her cup.

Something in her chest shifted.

That was the day she stopped hesitating. That was the day she truly began.

Three Years Later

Joy wrapped her hands around her tea cup, letting the warmth seep into her fingers. She had written her book in pieces, steeped in time and patience, just like the tea in front of her. A fragrant blend of citrus blossom and honeybush swirled in the steam, mirroring the lightness she felt in finally speaking her truth, unfiltered and free.

She glanced toward the window, where a small crowd gathered outside the bookstore next door. Her name was on the sign in the window. Her book, stacked neatly on the table inside.

She exhaled, a soft smile forming at the edges of her lips.

The Barista placed a delicate folded note beneath her cup, just as they always had.

She opened it carefully.

Joy let out a quiet laugh, shaking her head. Even now, the café knew just what to say.

She took a sip, letting the moment settle into her bones.

Then, she stood.

And she walked next door.

A Taste of Storyteller's Steam

Pour your truth with courage and grace

— Inspired by Citrus Bloom & Honeydrop: Honeybush, Orange Blossom, Calendula & Vanilla —

Mood Pairing: For when your truth rises gently but firmly ready to be shared, held, and heard.

Steep Time: Let it bloom at its own pace. Some truths take a moment to fully unfurl.

Body: Golden, floral, and quietly vibrant. Warm, steady, and softly awakening.

Origin: Brewed in honesty. Best sipped when you're ready to name what matters.

Color and Clarity

Bright golden-orange with a soft, glowing clarity—like light poured into a cup. It doesn't beg attention—it simply shines.

What story is rising within you, ready to be acknowledged or expressed?

____

____

____

Aroma

Orange blossom and calendula greet the senses with lightness. Vanilla grounds it in warmth. Honeybush adds depth without heaviness.

What does your story smell like? Bold? Gentle? Somewhere in between?

____

____

____

Flavor

Floral and citrus-forward with a velvety sweetness underneath. A sip that feels both illuminating and kind.

Where are you learning to express your story without shrinking or apologizing?

____

____

____

Fill in the blank: My truth is valid, even when ________________.

Aftertaste

A soft warmth that lingers—not to impress, but to stay rooted. It feels like alignment.

How would it feel to honor your story without needing to explain it?

____

____

____

Affirmation: I pour my truth with love, not fear. It's safe to be fully seen.

SIP 20: THE RICHER POUR

-Victoria-

The scent of clove and cinnamon curled through the air as Victoria stepped inside—familiar, grounding, and a little sharp, like the conversations they'd come to expect around this table. A slight flush rose to her cheeks from hurrying, the cool night air still clinging to her coat. She had lost track of time, again, and being late never sat well with her.

Scanning the room, she spotted her friends gathered in a corner booth, laughter bubbling between them. Jackson noticed her first and waved her over.

"Look who finally made it!" he teased.

She slid into her seat, shaking off the lingering rush of the day. Before she could even reach for the menu, Olivia pushed a folded napkin toward her.

"Check this out," she said, eyes bright with intrigue.

Victoria picked it up, her fingers tracing the handwritten words:

She exhaled, a small smile playing on her lips. A flash of memory, her mother at the kitchen table, sorting through unpaid bills, whispering promises that the next big break would change everything.

"The Barista gave it to us right before you arrived," Jackson explained, tilting his cup in salute toward the counter. "Perfect timing, as always, huh?"

Victoria nodded, absorbing the message. Tonight's gathering wasn't just a casual meetup, it was an unspoken tradition, a space where they openly discussed money, choices, and the small but powerful decisions shaping their financial security.

What had started as lighthearted grumbling about student loans years ago had grown into something deeper, honest conversations about inherited financial habits, struggles they faced, and wisdom they had gained along the way.

"So," Jackson leaned forward, fingers wrapped around his cup. "What's the one financial lesson you wish you'd learned sooner?"

Olivia chuckled. "That money isn't just about how much you make, it's about what you do with it. I used to think a bigger paycheck would solve everything, but lifestyle inflation is real. The more I made, the more I spent, without really thinking about what mattered."

She shook her head, a wry smile forming. "I remember my first real paycheck. I went straight to buy designer shoes. Not because I needed them, just because I could. And then I did it again, and again. I was earning more but feeling just as broke."

Victoria nodded as The Barista arrived and set a fresh cup in front of her with a welcoming smile before retreating to the counter. The tea's golden hue swirled in the steam, earthy, almost smoky. Victoria wrapped her hands around the warmth and breathed it in.

"That one hit me hard too," Victoria admitted. "Growing up, money was either feast or famine in my house. My parents chased big wins, lottery tickets, side hustles, bank loans, always believing the next stroke of luck would fix everything. But money isn't a rescue plan. It's a tool. I spent years unlearning that."

Caleb, usually the quiet one, spoke up. "I used to think ignoring my bank account meant I had one less thing to stress over," he admitted, rubbing the back of his neck. "But the anxiety never really went away. The numbers were still there, lurking in the background. The moment I actually sat down and faced them, I realized half the battle was in my head."

The Barista, who had been refilling cups in the background, joined the conversation. "You know, I once heard that money isn't just currency. It's energy. How we engage with it reflects how we engage with stability, security, and even self-worth."

Jackson raised an eyebrow. "Energy, huh?"

The Barista nodded. "Think about it. If you're constantly chasing money, it's like trying to brew a perfect cup of tea but never letting it steep. You're rushing, pouring too soon, never letting the full depth emerge. But if you approach it with intention, understanding your patterns, making thoughtful choices, you start to see it differently. More like a slow brew, something that builds over time."

Victoria let the words sink in as she sipped her tea. She had spent so many years untangling the financial habits she inherited, learning that wealth wasn't about sudden windfalls but about small, intentional decisions that built security.

She took another sip, the warmth of the tea reflecting the warmth of shared wisdom. Years ago, she might have brushed off this conversation, convinced that financial security was a game of luck, not strategy. But now, she saw it for what it was—a series of choices, deliberate and steady, shaping a life aligned with what truly mattered.

She was starting to feel at peace with her financial journey, not defined by past mistakes but shaped by what she was learning along the way.

She glanced around the table, listening. Money had once felt like a weight she carried alone, but being in this space, it felt lighter, something to navigate, not fear.

A Taste of Intention

Defining wealth for yourself

— Inspired by Turmeric, Roasted Dandelion Root, Cardamom & Oat Milk —

Mood Pairing: For when you're ready to receive more—of what fills, fuels, and affirms you.

Steep Time: Let it simmer with intention. The richness deepens with time and care.

Body: Earthy, spiced, and creamy. A warming blend that grounds and uplifts.

Origin: Brewed in self-worth. Best sipped when you're reclaiming your right to feel full—in presence, joy, and purpose.

Color and Clarity

Golden and opaque—like liquid sunlight with roots. You can't see through it, but you can feel its depth.

Where in your life are you being invited to receive more—to pour into yourself more richly, more fully?

Aroma

Spiced earthiness rises first—turmeric and dandelion root—followed by warm cardamom and the creaminess of oat milk. It smells like intention. Like a deep exhale.

What spaces or rituals remind you of your own richness?

____

____

____

Flavor

Full and rounded. Spice meets earth, softened by oat milk's cream. A blend that speaks of rootedness and rising all at once.

What would it feel like to give yourself the richest version of what you're craving—not the bare minimum?

____

____

____

Fill in the blank: I am no longer settling for ____________________.

Aftertaste

Lingering warmth with a touch of sweetness.
Not just comfort—but claiming.

What's one way you can pour into yourself today with intention and generosity?

____

____

____

Affirmation: I am rooted. I am ready. I receive the richness I deserve.

SIP 21: A GENTLE INFUSION OF MEMORIES

-Elaine-

The café was filled with the soft hum of instrumental music, a gentle current weaving through the quiet focus of the room. It was a *silent writing party*, a space where words flowed in shared solitude, where the only expectation was to sit, sip, and write.

Elaine slid into a seat by the window; her journal tucked under her arm. Around her, others were already settling in, flipping open notebooks, typing quietly, fingers hovering over pages in thought. The air buzzed with the energy of creation, even in silence.

A soft chime signaled the start of the session. The host, a woman with silver-streaked curls and an ever-present warm smile, dimmed the lights just slightly, as if lowering the volume of the outside world.

After briefly watching the Barista serve tea, Elaine exhaled, pressing the tip of her pen to the page.

But the words didn't come.

Not yet at least.

Her tea now beside her, she lifted her cup instead, inhaling the scent of turmeric and ginger. A blend she recognized instantly. It was grounding, earthy, the kind of tea that felt like a steadying hand on the shoulder.

Beside the cup, a folded note rested against the rim, just like always. Excited to see what today's message was, she picked it up and read.

Elaine read the message twice, her fingers tracing the paper's soft creases.

She knew this was true. She had always believed in the power of words, the way they could shape a memory, soften a sharp edge, bring clarity to something that felt impossible to hold. But lately, journaling had felt different. Harder.

It wasn't that she had nothing to say. If anything, there was *too much* to say.

The words sat at the edges of her mind, scattered fragments waiting to be sorted.

She took a slow sip of tea, letting the warmth settle deep in her chest.

Maybe she didn't need to make sense of everything at once. Maybe the words didn't have to come in perfect order. Maybe they just had to come.

She turned to a blank page.

And started writing.

A chime rang softly, signaling the end of the session.

Slowly, the quiet spell lifted, and the room stirred to life. Chairs shifted, pages were flipped closed, and the low murmur of voices filled the space.

Elaine stretched her fingers, rolling her shoulders. Around her, participants exchanged knowing smiles, an unspoken understanding that they had just shared something intimate, even in silence.

The host, standing near the counter, clapped her hands gently. "How did it go? Anyone feel like sharing?"

There was a pause, then a young woman with dark-rimmed glasses spoke up. "I started writing about my grandmother. It just… spilled out. I didn't expect that." She gave a small laugh, tucking her hair behind her ear. "I haven't thought about her in a while, but somehow, here she was."

A few nods of recognition followed.

A man at the far end of the table chuckled. "I thought I was going to work on my novel. Instead, I wrote about my childhood summers in Colorado." He shook his head, smiling. "Guess I had a few things to unpack."

Elaine felt the note still resting beside her. She turned it over in her hands before speaking.

"I wrote about memories too," she admitted. "Not just the happy ones, but the ones that feel unfinished." She hesitated, then added, "But writing about them made me realize, they don't have to be tied up in a perfect bow to be meaningful."

The host smiled. "That's the beauty of this space. Sometimes, we sit down to write one thing and discover something entirely different."

More murmurs of agreement filled the air. Someone raised their cup in a small toast, and laughter rippled through the group.

Elaine glanced down at her journal, her words still fresh on the page.

She had come here unsure, tangled in her own hesitation. But the words had come. They always did.

And tonight, she had welcomed them.

A Taste of Remembrance

The echo of what once was

— Inspired by Golden Embrace: Turmeric & Ginger Herbal Infusion —

Mood Pairing: For when memories stir quietly and tenderly, asking only to be felt, not fixed.

Steep Time: Let it steep gently. Memory doesn't rush, it returns when it's ready.

Body: Warm, soft, and grounding. A golden blend that holds you steady even as you remember.

Origin: Brewed in reflection. Best sipped when you're revisiting something tender.

Color and Clarity

Sunset gold. Not crystal clear, but glowing with emotion and warmth.

Which memory has been visiting you lately—and what is it trying to offer?

____

____

____

Aroma

Turmeric's earthy comfort rises first, followed by ginger's subtle spice. It smells like healing in motion.

What scent carries you back to a moment or person you're grateful for?

____

____

____

Flavor

Smooth with a gentle heat. Turmeric grounds, ginger lifts, and together they create a quiet strength. A sip that doesn't demand attention—it offers it.

What feeling or truth is still steeping beneath the memory?

____

____

____

Fill in the blank: I don't need to fix the past—I just need to _______.

Aftertaste

A calm warmth that sits low and stays long. Like a hand on your back. Like a familiar song.

What memory brings you comfort—not because it's perfect, but because it's part of you?

____

____

____

Affirmation: I hold my memories with love. I let them shape me, not define me.

SIP 22: INFUSED INTENTION

-Maggie-

Some visits begin before anyone arrives. They unfold in the space between, planned, imagined, and deeply felt.

Maggie tapped her pen thoughtfully against her notebook, gazing out the café window. Sunlight filtered through the leaves, casting soft, shifting shadows across her table.

She was planning for her niece Emily's upcoming visit, the kind that lived on the calendar like a star. Maggie's notebook was already filling with color-coded lists and doodled hearts, tiny arrows pointing to ideas like *"rooftop picnic?"* and *"Broadway matinee!"* Scribbled between the lines were reminders to pick up Emily's favorite pastries and scout out a good photo spot near the park fountain.

Her phone buzzed. A new message from Emily lit up the screen—*"What if we try that museum with the giant treehouse exhibit?"*

Maggie grinned. All morning, they'd been texting back and forth, trading links, voice notes, and emoji-filled excitement. Museums, parks, bakery menus, each message felt like another brushstroke in the memory they were building together, even before the visit began.

Maggie smiled, imagining Emily's excitement mirroring her own. These small exchanges, the "what about this place?" texts, the quick emojis, felt like more than logistics. They were little love notes unfolding in real time, a quiet reminder that presence isn't measured in length, but in depth.

"Planning something special?" came a warm, familiar voice.

Maggie looked up to see The Barista standing beside her, a fresh cup of tea in hand, a golden chamomile blend infused with vanilla and cinnamon. Their expression held the kind of knowing that came from more than observation.

Maggie laughed softly, shaking her head. "I didn't realize it showed."

The Barista placed the tea gently beside her notebook and offered a kind smile. "Sometimes it's not about how much time we get, it's how present we are in the time we have."

Maggie inhaled the comforting aroma of cinnamon and vanilla, letting the warmth settle in her chest. "I guess I've been so focused on planning the big moments… I forget how much meaning lives in the small ones."

"Then let this remind you," The Barista said, placing a napkin on the table. It read:

Maggie grinned, placing the napkin beside her notebook. She wrapped her hands around the warm cup, letting the steam rise and wrap around her like a familiar embrace. The blend, chamomile laced with vanilla and a whisper of cinnamon, carried a softness that reminded her of bedtime stories, quiet check-ins, and the kind of love that doesn't rush. It was comfort brewed into something tangible.

As The Barista moved on, her gaze drifted back to her notes. She could already picture it, Emily's bright eyes lighting up as they explored the city together: stopping by her favorite bakery, sharing sweet pastries, laughing over a spilled cup of tea, and swapping stories in the park.

Her heart softened. She didn't need to be present at every family gathering to hold an important place in their lives. It was the small gestures, the handwritten letter in the mailbox, the voice memo filled with laughter, the custom tea blend she'd made just for them, that built a bridge across the miles.

Emily's voice echoed in her mind from a recent call: "You always answer when I call. Even when I don't say much, you just… get it. That means more than I can explain."

Opening her notes app, Maggie began typing, sparked by a sudden clarity: an afternoon exploring museums, an evening Broadway show, baking cookies, and creating stories Emily would carry home like tucked-away souvenirs.

A quiet warmth spread through her as she wrote, grounding her in a deeper truth, love wasn't bound by proximity. It lived in the spaces between calls, in the planning, the laughter, the choosing to show up even from afar.

Maggie closed her notebook and took another sip. The trip would be beautiful, yes, but even this, the planning, had become its own kind of memory.

A quiet reminder: *love lives in the little things.* She picked up her pen again, heart light and steady.

A Taste of Meaning

The small ways love endures

— Inspired by Chamomile, Vanilla & Cinnamon Herbal Blend —

Mood Pairing: For when you want to be exactly where you are, not ahead, not behind, just here.

Steep Time: Let it steep longer than usual. Presence isn't hurried, it's honored.

Body: Soft, warm, and slightly sweet. A cozy blend that whispers, "You're doing just fine."

Origin: Brewed in awareness. Best sipped when you're learning to love the moment you're in.

Color and Clarity

Golden and calm. The kind of hue that feels like afternoon light on a slow day.

What beauty or truth is revealing itself when you stop rushing toward what's next?

____

____

____

Aroma

Soothing chamomile. A swirl of vanilla. Cinnamon hums beneath it all. It smells like a soft exhale.

What does presence feel like in your body when you allow it to arrive?

____

____

____

Flavor

A sip of gentle sweetness. Chamomile calms, vanilla rounds, cinnamon warms. No urgency. Just a moment held fully.

Where are you learning to sit with what is—instead of chasing what could be?

____

____

____

Fill in the blank: This moment may be quiet, but it still holds ________.

Aftertaste

A soft linger, like a thought you're not ready to let go of yet. It leaves you present, not pondering.

How can you celebrate presence today—not as a concept, but as a practice?

____

____

____

Affirmation: I honor the moment I'm in. There's richness here, even in the stillness.

SIP 23: THE STEADY POUR OF PRESENCE

-Kevin-

Fatherhood didn't come with a manual, but if it did, Kevin was pretty sure it would've skipped the chapter on grown daughters and ghosted text messages.

He'd spent years learning how to fix things, loose cabinet doors, bruised knees, the occasional broken heart. But nothing in his toolkit prepared him for this part: the waiting, the wondering, the silent shifts that came with distance.

The door to *The Authenticitea Café* opened with a soft chime, and Kevin stepped inside, shaking the damp chill from his jacket. The warmth of the café embraced him like an old memory—familiar and comforting, though he hadn't planned to be here today. His feet had simply carried him, as if they knew what he needed before his mind could catch up.

He settled into a corner booth, exhaling as he stared out the window. The rain streaked the glass in slow, meandering trails, mirroring the thoughts circling in his head. He didn't have much on the agenda today. With his girls now old enough to do their own thing, he often found himself with extra time, enough for spontaneous stops like this one at a tea café.

They were grown now. Confident. Independent. Moving through the world in ways that both amazed and terrified him. He had spent years preparing them for this, and yet, as he sat there, a hollow ache filled his chest. Was this what fatherhood became? A series of distant check-ins, the occasional text, the rare visit when schedules aligned?

He thought back to the early years—braiding tiny pigtails, bedtime stories that turned into giggle-fits, burnt pancakes on Saturday mornings. Love had been so simple then, effortless in its expression. Now, love looked like messages left on read, one-word replies, and the growing fear that maybe he had already become a background character in their lives.

A steaming cup of tea appeared before him, placed gently on the table along with a folded napkin. He hadn't ordered anything, but he knew how this place worked.

He hesitated before picking up the napkin, unfolding it with careful fingers.

He blinked, staring at the words as if they held the answer he hadn't realized he was seeking.

His throat tightened.

Presence. Had he been present enough?

Had they felt seen, truly seen, in the ways that mattered?

He lifted the cup, inhaling the scent, chamomile and rose. A blend for patience and open-heartedness. He smirked, shaking his head. *Yeah, that sounds about right.*

As he took his first sip, warmth spread through him, settling deep in his chest. Maybe that was the answer. Not pushing. Not expecting. Just being there, steady as ever, until they found their way back.

The café hummed around him, the gentle clink of cups, soft jazz playing low, a couple laughing near the counter. Life moved forward all around him, and yet here he sat, somewhere between memory and meaning.

He reached for his phone, thumb hovering over their names. He could send something simple. A "thinking of you." A meme. A photo of the tea. Something light enough not to feel intrusive, but real enough to say: *I'm still here.*

But instead, he set it down again.

It wasn't about what he sent. It was about how he showed up, subtle, consistent, and open. He'd always prided himself on being the problem-solver, the doer, the one who stepped in with answers. But maybe connection, at this stage, wasn't about fixing. Maybe it was about listening. Offering space. Letting them know the door was always open.

Kevin looked down at the tea again and chuckled. He could practically hear their voices teasing him about his "soft side."

They'd always joked he was the tough one. The "rules parent." But what they didn't see were the silent sacrifices. The nights he stood quietly in their doorways, watching their chest rise and fall in sleep, praying the world wouldn't bruise their softness. The way he memorized their favorite songs so he could play them in the car. The tears he swallowed during every milestone, proud, bittersweet, full.

Fatherhood had never been about being the loudest. It had been about presence, exactly as that napkin had said. Sometimes shown in whispers. In small gestures. In the consistency of showing up, even when words failed.

He took another sip.

Maybe it was time to tell them that. Not in a long speech, but in the same way he had always loved them: simply, quietly, truthfully.

He picked up his phone again. This time, he typed:

"Just drinking tea and thought of you. Miss your laugh."

He hit send before he could overthink it.

No expectations. Just presence.

A Taste of Presence

Align with what matters most

— Inspired by Chamomile & Rose Herbal Infusion —

Mood Pairing: For when you want to remain grounded, not as a reaction, but as a quiet declaration.

Steep Time: Let it steep without watching the clock. Presence grows stronger when it's unmeasured.

Body: Delicate but certain. Chamomile brings calm, rose offers open-hearted grace.

Origin: Brewed in intentional stillness. Best sipped when you're choosing to stay, especially when you could drift away.

Color and Clarity

Pale gold with a pink tint, like sunrise reflected in still water. Subtle, yet unmistakably there.

What space in your life is asking for more presence, and less performance?

____

____

____

Aroma

Chamomile's grounding hum meets the tender bloom of rose. It smells like a steady breath held with care.

What are you learning to stay with, even when it feels vulnerable?

____

____

____

Flavor

Gentle and floral. A quiet strength that unfolds sip by sip. No rush. Just presence that deepens with each taste.

Where are you allowing yourself to stay with what's real—rather than escaping into what's next?

____

____

____

Fill in the blank: I am learning that presence is not passive—it is ________.

Aftertaste

Soft but sustaining. A warm reminder that staying with yourself is its own kind of bravery.

What anchors you when things feel uncertain—but you choose to remain grounded anyway?

____

____

____

Affirmation: I stay with myself. I am present, even in the quiet moments.

A Pause to Sip: Between Connection & Healing

Some moments stay with us, while others must be released, making space for what truly nourishes.

A Cup of Healing

Leaning into letting go, honoring what was, and stepping into your next chapter.

SIP 24: THE FIRST SIP OF SOMETHING NEW

-June and Mike-

June and Mike sat at a table near the window, though they hadn't been here in a while. The space felt unchanged, the same polished oak table, the same hanging shelves lined with ceramic cups, colorful books, and glass jars of loose-leaf blends. Yet, for them, everything was different.

The Authenticitea Café was quieter than usual this morning, only a few customers lingered in about, their voices hushed, the occasional clink of a spoon against porcelain filling the silence. Sunlight stretched through the large windows, casting long golden streaks across the wooden floors.

The Barista approached, placing two steaming cups in front of them without a word. June reached for hers, inhaling the warmth, expecting the familiar comfort of chamomile. But something was different. She took a sip, her brow furrowing slightly at the unexpected notes, earthier, bolder, with a hint of citrus.

"This isn't what I was expecting," she muttered, glancing at Mike, who had already taken a sip of his own.

He nodded, setting his cup down with a small, curious frown. Before either of them could say anything, The Barista caught their eye from across the counter, offering a knowing smile.

"A new blend," they called over. "Sometimes, change finds us before we're ready for it."

June looked down at the tea, watching the steam curl into the air. The words, *"a new blend"* settled in a way she couldn't quite name.

Then she saw it, a small, folded napkin tucked beneath her cup. How could she have forgotten about this café ritual? She picked it up, smoothing the paper-thin creases with her fingertips.

In delicate, looping script, it read:

Neither of them spoke for a long time. June traced the edge of her cup with one finger, her other hand still resting on the napkin, as if anchoring herself to the words.

Mike exhaled heavily, his gaze distant. "One day, we were picking out names. The next, we were being told to let go of something we hadn't even had the chance to hold."

June swallowed, her throat tight. The grief had been sharp in those first few weeks, an ache that sat heavy on her chest, an emptiness that stretched through the spaces where hope had once lived. But as time passed, the sorrow had softened, not gone, but settled, reshaped into something quieter.

Through the café window, she noticed a mother kneeling in front of a small child, tying their shoelaces before they continued their stroll. A moment of care, of tenderness. She expected the familiar ache, the pull of what may never be. But instead, something else stirred inside her. Not absence. Not longing. Just… something lighter.

Mike must have noticed her watching.

"I used to think letting go meant losing something," he murmured, turning back to her. "But maybe it just means carrying it differently."

She met his gaze, warmth flickering behind her sorrow. "Maybe."

His fingers curled over hers, a familiar gesture, steady and sure.

A quiet shift in the air made June look up.

Jared, a neighbor they've exchanged a few kind but brief conversations with was approaching their table, his steps unhurried, as if debating whether to stop.

"Hey," Jared said, voice steadying. "Good to see you both."

June looked up, smiling warmly but with an edge of something unreadable in her eyes. "Jared, hey. You doing alright?"

Jared nodded, slow and measured. "Trying to be. You two?"

Mike glanced at June before answering. "Same."

Jared didn't press, just offered a small, warm smile. "See you around."

As he walked away, the silence he left behind felt different—not heavier, not lighter, just there.

Mike turned back to June, searching her expression. "Do you think we'll ever get past this?"

June let out a slow breath, lifting her cup to her lips before answering. "I don't know," she admitted. "But I know we'll keep going. And I know that doesn't mean we've failed."

Mike squeezed her hand, nodding. The thought had crossed both their minds more than once, whether their story would always feel incomplete without a child, whether they could still build something whole and meaningful together.

"Maybe being parents isn't our path," he said quietly. "Maybe it never was."

June held his gaze, searching for the pain that used to sit behind his words. It was still there, but something else had taken root, too, acceptance, maybe. Or at least the beginning of it.

She took another sip, starting to get used to this new blend.

"And that's okay," she whispered.

Mike's gaze drifted toward the wooden shelves near the counter. A small tin of tea sat among the others, its label scrawled in delicate handwriting: *New Beginnings.*

He stood without thinking, grabbed the tin, and set it on the table between them.

"Maybe we should try something different," he said.

June studied it, then him. Slowly, she nodded.

A breeze stirred through the open door as another customer entered, carrying with it the scent of outside mingling with the café's—earthy, sun-warmed concrete, fresh air, the faint aroma of steeping tea, and the quiet promise of something just beginning.

June glanced at the tin again, then at Mike.

They didn't know what came next.

And they didn't have to.

She reached for her cup, took another sip, and let the new flavor settle inside her.

A Taste of Soft Beginnings

Honor loss as a quiet guide toward what's next

— Inspired by Green Tea, Orange Peel, Ginger Root & a Hint of Smokey Lapsang —

Mood Pairing: For when you're stepping into something new, not without fear, but with hope lit anyway.

Steep Time: Let it steep long enough to awaken but not overwhelm. The start is tender.

Body: Earthy, citrus-bright, and lightly smoky. A grounding brew with flickers of lift.

Origin: Brewed at the edge of change. Best sipped when you're opening a new chapter.

Color and Clarity

Muted green with amber edges, like dawn breaking through mist. A quiet shift from what was into what's becoming.

What are you beginning to believe is possible again?

____

____

____

Aroma

Crisp green tea meets the bright lift of orange. Ginger and smoke follow, grounding, protective, honest.

What does this new chapter smell like to you—fresh? familiar? full of possibility?

____

____

____

Flavor

Bright citrus meets earthy depth. Ginger adds spark, and smoke holds memory. A sip that feels like looking ahead while honoring where you've been.

What part of your past are you taking with you into this new beginning—and what are you choosing to leave behind?

____

____

____

Fill in the blank: I am stepping forward with ________________________.

Aftertaste

Lingering clarity with a grounded warmth. Not a clean slate, but a clearer one.

How would it feel to welcome this new beginning, even if it's uncertain?

____

____

____

Affirmation: I greet what's next with open hands. Every beginning is a return to trust.

SIP 25: HEALING IN SMALL SIPS

-Jordan-

Tracing the scar on his knuckles, Jordan let his fingers linger over the faint ridge, a ghost of an old emotion flickering in his memory. It hadn't been intentional. It was just where his frustration landed.

The weight of the day clung to him as he sank into his usual seat, exhaling slowly. The warmth of *The Authenticitea Café* wrapped around him, a quiet contrast to the cold that still lingered on his skin. He rolled his shoulders, rubbing his hands together to chase away the chill.

A few moments passed before The Barista appeared, setting a cup in front of him along with a folded napkin. A welcoming nod, a familiar smile. No words, just the quiet offering he had come to expect in this place.

He smirked, shaking his head as he unfolded the note.

The smirk faded. His fingers pressed into the paper as his throat tightened.

The Barista returned to his table, their presence as steady as ever. "Chamomile and licorice root," they said. "For healing."

Jordan exhaled slowly, picking up the cup. "You always know," he said before taking a sip.

As the Barista stepped away, a movement caught his eye.

Near the window, a kid sat curled into the corner of a chair, hoodie pulled up over his head, fingers absently tapping against an empty cup.

Something about him tugged at Jordan's memory.

Then, the boy shifted, and Jordan's breath stalled.

Thin face. Too-big hoodie. Shoulders curled inward like he was bracing for something unseen.

Jordan knew him.

Because the kid was him.

"You staring at me for a reason?" The boy's voice had that familiar edge—defensive, wary, like he was used to people looking but not seeing.

Jordan swallowed, leaning forward. "Just wondering why you're here."

The kid shrugged, his fingers tightening around his cup. "I dunno. Just ended up here, I guess."

Jordan inhaled sharply. He remembered this version of himself, the kid who never got to choose where he ended up.

"Things don't always stay the same," Jordan said carefully.

The boy scoffed, kicking at the leg of the chair. "Yeah, they do. You just get better at pretending they don't."

Jordan's chest tightened. He knew that feeling.

At ten, he had packed a suitcase in under ten minutes, stuffing his favorite sweatshirt into his backpack because his mom had woken him before dawn, whispering, *We have to go.* He never asked why. Just climbed into the car and stared out the window, counting streetlights.

By twelve, he had learned how to read a room before stepping inside. Some of the men in his mother's life were kind. Others… less so. None stayed long enough for him to feel settled.

His dad was states away, his presence reduced to rare brief visits and phone calls that always ended too soon. When the line clicked dead, Jordan would sit on his bed, gripping the receiver long after the dial tone faded, wondering why it never lasted long enough.

There had been moments—*so many moments*—where it would've been easier to let anger take over. To slip into the same choices some of the other boys in his neighborhood had made.

But something inside him resisted. Maybe it was the way his mom kept trying, even when she had nothing left. Maybe it was knowing that if he let go completely, he might not find his way back.

So, he made different choices. Not perfect ones, but better ones.

Now, looking at the younger version of himself sitting across the table, Jordan saw it, the weight of time pressing down on small shoulders, the quiet fight to hold everything together.

And for the first time, he wanted to tell the kid the one thing he had always needed to hear.

Jordan placed his hand on the folded napkin.

The kid frowned as he slid it across the table. Slowly, he picked it up, unfolding it with cautious fingers.

The boy's grip tightened on the napkin, his jaw shifting. "Who wrote this?"

Jordan didn't answer. He just watched as the kid swallowed hard, shoving the napkin into his hoodie pocket like something solid to hold onto.

After a long moment, the boy pushed back his chair. "I should go," he mumbled, standing abruptly.

Jordan didn't stop him. He only nodded. "You'll be okay."

The kid hesitated for half a second before turning and walking toward the door. As he stepped through, Jordan caught a glimpse of something familiar, the same stubborn resilience he'd carried all those years ago.

And just like that, he was gone.

"You okay?" The Barista's voice was gentle, but certain.

Jordan blinked, the café settling back into its usual rhythm. The chair across from him was empty. The only thing left was his cup of tea and the faint trace of his own reflection in the window.

He let out a breath. "Yeah. Just… thinking."

The Barista tilted their head slightly, "Looking back, do you see it now?"

Jordan nodded, setting his tea down. "Yeah. It's just… back then, it felt endless."

"Pain has a way of making time feel heavy. But even the hardest moments pass. And you? You chose to move forward. That's something worth honoring."

Jordan's fingers curled around his cup.

He had moved forward. He had built a life: a career, a home, friendships that weren't based on survival but on trust.

For years, he had wondered if the kid he used to be, would be proud of the man he became.

Now, for the first time, he knew the answer.

A Taste of Mending Light

Noticing your healing in the quietest moments

— Inspired by Chamomile & Licorice Root Herbal Infusion —

Mood Pairing: For when you're in the middle of the healing, not fixed, but faithfully continuing.

Steep Time: Steep with patience. The full flavor of healing only emerges with time and stillness.

Body: Soft and nurturing. Chamomile cradles the heart; licorice root brings a quiet sweetness that lingers.

Origin: Brewed in renewal. Best sipped when you're tending to tender places.

Color and Clarity

Light golden, soft and clear. Like sunlight filtering through a sheer curtain. Gentle doesn't mean weak, it means attuned.

Where are you being asked to be gentle with yourself right now?

____

____

____

Aroma

Soothing and slightly sweet. Chamomile leads with calm; licorice hums beneath like quiet encouragement. It smells like the warmth of a hand on your back.

What brings you comfort when the healing feels slow?

____

____

____

Flavor

A mellow blend of familiar calm and soft sweetness. A sip that doesn't ask you to be okay—just to keep sipping.

Where in your life are you offering yourself grace instead of pressure?

____

____

____

Fill in the blank: *My healing doesn't have to be fast. It just has to _______.*

Aftertaste

A slow warmth that expands gently. Not fixing—restoring. Not erasing—integrating.

What part of your story are you learning to hold with tenderness instead of judgment?

____

____

____

Affirmation: I am healing, one breath, one sip, one moment at a time.

SIP 26: A CUP OF SECOND CHANCES

-Lucy-

Lucy stepped into *The Authenticitea Café* as a cold breeze clung to her heels, nudging her forward before she felt ready to move. Her hands stayed buried in her coat pockets, shoulders hunched, not just from the winter air, but from the invisible weight of a life in transition.

The warmth and quiet hum of conversations wrapped around her like a reassuring embrace, but the comfort felt distant, as though her heart wasn't quite ready to accept it.

Her footsteps carried a heaviness she'd become accustomed to, weighed down by the reality she'd been living lately. She had just dropped her children off at the house that once felt like a forever home, the place she decorated with care, where birthday parties had filled rooms with laughter, and where family movie nights were a cherished routine.

Now, it was merely a place she visited, a constant reminder of the family life she no longer had. Her divorce rearranged everything, leaving her feeling disconnected, at times angry as she floated between two worlds, neither of which felt entirely like home.

This café stop was a brief interlude on her way to therapy, another crucial anchor in her new reality. Therapy had become a sanctuary of its own, a place where she could freely unravel her tangled emotions and begin stitching herself back together.

Today, especially, she needed a moment to gather herself before facing another session, unsure how to navigate the maze of emotions that lingered after dropping off her kids.

She chose a corner table away from curious eyes, sinking into a chair that creaked softly beneath her. The café was a temporary shelter from the loneliness that echoed off the walls of her small apartment, walls that felt too empty without her children's laughter.

Lucy scanned the table for the menu, already dismissing the thought of a latte. Her budget was tight, another stark reminder of how life had changed. Water with lemon had become her quiet act of resilience, a small choice that reminded her she was still standing, still moving forward despite everything she'd lost.

Settling deeper into her chair, Lucy noticed the soft clink on the table. A steaming cup, aromatic and unfamiliar, appeared before her. She didn't need to taste it to know it was something floral, maybe rose, with a trace of something citrusy beneath. Surprised and slightly annoyed, she looked up to meet The Barista's gentle eyes. She had hoped today she might slip in unnoticed, hidden from the café's usual insightful gestures.

"I didn't order this," the words came sharper than she intended because even the smallest, unexpected gesture was one more thing out of her control.

The Barista smiled, a subtle acknowledgment, before turning away.

Lucy eyed the folded napkin beneath the cup skeptically, then unfolded it to reveal neatly handwritten words:

Her first reaction was irritation. The simplistic optimism felt almost dismissive of her pain, the complexity of her loss.

She didn't want platitudes or easy solutions. Her therapist had told her healing was messy, imperfect, and deeply personal. But as she stared at the words again, their truth began to gently press against the edges of her resistance.

She took a reluctant sip of the tea, its warmth spreading comfortingly despite her reluctance. Lucy knew she wasn't ready to fully embrace The Barista's wisdom, not yet. But perhaps, like her therapy sessions, these small moments were nudging her toward seeing possibilities she couldn't yet imagine.

Lucy breathed deeply, allowing herself a cautious openness. She knew she wasn't going to solve anything today, but perhaps she could find just enough courage to carry her forward; to therapy, to healing, and ultimately, to whatever new beginnings lay beyond her current pain.

With quiet resolve, she finished the last sip of tea, tucked the napkin's quote into her notebook, and rose from the table, ready to face the next step in her journey.

A Taste to Carry Forward

Honor what was and invite what's next

— Inspired by Rose Petals, Chamomile, Honeybush & Lemon Balm —

Mood Pairing: For when you're rebuilding, not from perfection, but from permission.

Steep Time: Let it steep slowly. This isn't about rushing to repair, it's about gently returning.

Body: Delicate and restorative. Floral with a grounding sweetness and a citrus lift.

Origin: Brewed in humility and hope. Best sipped when you're learning to love what's still becoming.

Color and Clarity

A soft blush pink with warm gold undertones. Like light seen through forgiveness. Clear enough to reflect, gentle enough to soothe.

What are you beginning again, with more compassion this time?

____

____

____

Aroma

Rose and chamomile rise first—familiar, floral, tender. Honeybush adds warmth. Lemon balm brightens what was heavy.

What part of your story is ready to be held with gentler hands?

____

____

____

Flavor

Floral, mellow, and a touch citrusy. A brew that doesn't ask for perfection—just presence.

Where in your life are you offering yourself a second chance?

____

____

____

Fill in the blank: I don't need to get it right the first time to _______.

Aftertaste

A quiet sweetness that stays. The kind of taste that reminds you not of what was lost, but of what can still be found.

What would it feel like to fully receive the second chances being offered to you—by life, others, or yourself?

____

____

____

Affirmation: I forgive myself forward. I welcome the beauty of beginning again.

SIP 27: SPILLING THE TEA

-Jared-

The morning light spilled through the windows as the door to *The Authenticitea Café* swung open, carrying the weight of a decision not yet spoken.

Jared stepped inside, shoulders squared but heart hammering beneath his ribcage. The scent of honey and spices curled around him, wrapping him in a warmth he wasn't sure he deserved today.

Lately, this café had become the talk of the town, and after a quick stop here once before, he understood why. It was known as a place where people found clarity, where unspoken truths steeped like tea leaves, coaxed into something easier to swallow.

He didn't come here on a whim. The first time he entered *The Authenticitea Café*, it had been an accident, or at least that's what he had told himself.

He saw Zack through the window, a friend he hadn't caught up with in a while. Jared had walked in to say a quick hello, and on his way out, he grabbed a tea to go. The Barista handed him a folded napkin with his drink. The message had lingered in his mind for days.

Jared read the words the moment he stepped outside. He let out a quiet chuckle, shaking his head, as if the universe itself was waiting for him to catch up. But later, in the quiet of his home, he unfolded the napkin again and again, tracing the ink as if it held the weight of the decision he wasn't ready to face. It was enough to bring him back here, today, when he finally admitted to himself that the truth was no longer something he could ignore. Now that he knew it, he had to let others know—most importantly, his wife.

He hesitated by the counter, running a hand through his hair before ordering an iced tea, something crisp, something grounding. The Barista, ever knowing, offered him a small smile. "You're back," they said, sliding the cool glass toward him. "Peach hibiscus. For clarity."

Jared swallowed hard and carried the cup to a quiet corner. Coming here was not part of the plan, not today. But sitting in his car, staring at the home he shared with his wife, the weight of unspoken words had settled so heavily on his chest that he feared he might never breathe again. And so, he drove, not toward answers, but away from the paralysis of inaction.

He liked women. He loved his wife. –But he also liked men.

And in the quiet moments when he allowed himself to be honest, he realized that those feelings weren't something he could push aside any longer. They weren't fleeting thoughts or passing curiosities. They were real, and they were reshaping everything he thought he knew about himself.

He spent so much of his life believing he was one thing, that the life he built fit the person he was supposed to be.

A husband.

A partner.

A man who followed the rules, did what was expected, never questioned the path he was on.

But now, the path had changed. Or maybe, it had always been different, and he was just now seeing it clearly.

He took a slow sip of his tea, letting the coolness settle him, but the tightness in his chest remained.

How did he tell her?

How did he say the words that would change their lives forever?

His phone buzzed on the table. He stared at the screen, his wife's name glowing back at him. First a text:

Where are you? Don't forget we have plans.

Then, before he could respond, his phone rang. He hesitated, letting it ring once. Twice. Then he pressed decline.

He couldn't pretend anymore. He couldn't ignore the truth because it was inconvenient or painful.

The truth was that he wasn't just a man who liked men. He was a man who couldn't see himself staying married to his wife while knowing that part of himself existed. It wasn't fair to her. It wasn't fair to him.

And then there was his family. His friends. The people who had only ever known him as the version of himself he had worked so hard to present.

What would they say?

Would they understand?

Would they turn away?

He had no answers, only questions that circled his mind like an unrelenting storm.

He traced the rim of the glass with his thumb, inhaling the faint floral scent. Maybe he didn't need to figure it all out today. Maybe, for now, it was enough to sit here, sip his tea, and allow himself the space to acknowledge that he was on the brink of something new.

A soft clink at a table nearby drew his attention. Then he glanced down at his table and saw a folded napkin, was sitting beside his drink. He didn't notice it before, but the message was unmistakably meant for him.

Jared let out a breath, a hint of something lighter pressing against his chest. He ran his fingers over the ink, letting the words settle into him.

As he gathered his belongings, preparing to leave, he caught a glimpse of his his neighbors, June and Mike. Something about the way they leaned into each other, the weight behind their low conversation, told him he wasn't the only one carrying something heavy. On impulse, he approached their table, nodding in greeting.

"Hey," he said, voice steadying. "Good to see you both."

June looked up first, smiling warmly but with an edge of something unreadable in her eyes. "Jared, hey. You doing alright?"

He nodded slowly. "Trying to be. You two?"

Mike glanced at June before answering. "Same."

Jared didn't press, just offered a small, knowing smile. "See you around."

June gave his arm a gentle squeeze as he turned to leave, while Mike lifted his cup in a small, silent toast. As Jared stepped outside, the morning air met him with a crisp clarity, a reminder that, whatever came next, he wasn't the only one figuring it out.

A Taste of Revelation

Saying what needs to be said

— Inspired by Peach Hibiscus Clarity: Iced Herbal Blend —

Mood Pairing: For when truth bubbles to the surface, and you're ready to say it, share it, or sip it boldly.

Steep Time: Steep chilled and steep true. Best served with courage, not heat.

Body: Bright, bold, and refreshing. Hibiscus gives tang. Peach adds sweetness. Together, they zing with clarity.

Origin: Brewed in honesty. Best sipped when truth becomes a release, not a weapon.

Color and Clarity

Vibrant pink-red, like a sunset with something to say. Bold. Clear. Impossible to ignore.

What truth is rising that you've been trying to dilute or hold in too long?

____

____

____

Aroma

Fruity and floral, with tart edges and soft sweetness. It smells like boldness held with care.

What does honesty smell like to you? Sharp? Sweet? Liberating?

___

___

___

Flavor

Zesty hibiscus and juicy peach strike a sharp-sweet balance. It hits first, and then refreshes. Like truth, when spoken with heart.

Where are you ready to be more real—with yourself or someone else?

___

___

___

Fill in the blank: I can be honest and still be ____________________.

Aftertaste

A tangy linger with a clean finish.

Truth, when served with grace, leaves you lighter.

What truth are you ready to pour, not to stir drama, but to clear space for what's real?

___

___

___

Affirmation: *I speak truth with love. I sip boldly and breathe easier after.*

SIP 28: A BREW OF REFLECTION

-Paige-

Paige adjusted her glasses and stared at the page, but the words refused to stay still. Around her, books whispered their stories to readers who seemed to understand them with ease. She wanted that. She had always wanted that.

The *Drop Everything and Read (D.E.A.R) Party* at *The Authentic-itea Café* was well underway, the soft hum of turning pages and the occasional clink of teacups filling the cozy space. Warm light pooled around the mismatched tables, and the scent of steeping tea leaves curled through the air like a gentle embrace.

Everyone around her seemed at ease, lost in their books, their eyes moving effortlessly across the pages. Meanwhile, Paige sat frozen, her breath caught somewhere between hesitation and frustration.

She wasn't reading.

Not in the way she wished she could.

In her lap was a novel she had been wanting to read for months, one she had picked up and put down more times than she could count. But this time, she had come prepared. Beneath her sweater, hidden behind the loose curl of her hair, was a single wireless earbud.

The narrator's voice hummed softly in her ear, reading the words aloud as her eyes followed along.

Immersive reading, they called it. A way to bridge the gap, to strengthen the connection between what she heard and what she saw. It was supposed to help, to make reading feel *possible*.

But even with the soft narration guiding her, the familiar tightness in her chest remained.

Her gaze flickered around the room. No one was watching her. No one cared how she was reading. And yet, shame pressed against her ribs like a weight she had carried for years.

She had spent a lifetime finding ways to hide her struggle, skimming pages, memorizing opening lines, nodding through book discussions. She wanted more. She wanted to hold a book in her hands and *read* it, word by word, on her own.

A cup of tea appeared beside her, the delicate porcelain clicking softly against the saucer. Paige looked up to see *The Barista*, their presence steady, their eyes warm with understanding.

They didn't say anything. Didn't press.

Instead, they slipped a folded napkin onto the saucer before walking away.

Paige hesitated, then picked it up with careful fingers, unfolding the neatly creased square.

She swallowed, her eyes tracing the letters. She knew the words, recognized most of them, but they blurred slightly, her mind stuttering over the sentence, her confidence unraveling.

She glanced toward the counter, where The Barista was adjusting a tray of teacups. A beat of indecision passed. Then, with a steadying breath, she removed her earbud, set her book aside, and stood.

The café still buzzed with quiet energy, the sound of pages turning filling the air. No one noticed as she approached the counter.

The Barista looked up, a small smile forming as Paige hesitated.

"I, um…" Paige exhaled, holding up the napkin. "Could you… read this with me?"

For a moment, she felt exposed—raw, like she had peeled back a layer of herself she had spent years keeping hidden.

But The Barista didn't flinch. Didn't react with surprise or pity.

Instead, they nodded, took the napkin, and placed it between them on the counter.

"Of course," they said gently. "Let's read it together."

Paige's throat tightened.

The Barista pointed to the first word, waiting for her. Paige inhaled, then slowly, carefully, began to sound it out.

*"Growth… "*she started, a word she knew, though it didn't come easily.

The Barista nodded in quiet encouragement.

Paige took another breath.

"Is the… courage…—"

The words came slower than she wanted, but they came. And for the first time in a long time, she let herself believe that was enough.

Warmth spread through her chest, not just from the tea, but from something deeper.

She looked up and met The Barista's eyes.

They smiled.

Before returning to her seat, Paige smiled back.

A Taste of Gentle Acceptance

Stillness as a strength

— Inspired by White Tea, Chamomile & Linden Flower —

Mood Pairing: For when you're ready to reflect, not react, and anchor into what's true for you.

Steep Time: Give it time. Let the quiet unfold its layers slowly.

Body: Light but rooted. Floral, soft, and gently affirming.

Origin: Brewed in inner steadiness. Best sipped when you're choosing pause over performance.

Color and Clarity

Pale gold with a hint of silver. Clear, calm, and understated. The kind of clarity that doesn't demand attention—it invites it.

What recent experience is asking to be seen through stiller eyes?

____

____

____

Aroma

Chamomile rises first, soothing and warm, then linden flower follows with its delicate sweetness. The white tea anchors it in quiet presence.

What emotion or insight has quietly lingered, waiting to be named?

____

____

____

Flavor

Gentle and layered. A soft introduction with a quietly strong center. It's a sip that reminds you to keep listening—even to the parts of yourself that whisper.

What is reflection revealing that action may have overlooked?

____

____

____

Fill in the blank: I don't have to be loud to be ____________________.

Aftertaste

Soft, steady calm. The kind that settles in your bones and stays a while. Less of a finish—more of a companion.

What are you learning to carry with softness instead of urgency?

____

____

____

Affirmation: I trust the quiet within me. My strength grows in stillness.

SIP 29: THE ESSENCE OF CHANGE

-Lily-

She'd always imagined her first home would come with excitement, not a mild existential crisis.

Lily stepped out of the car, real estate brochure clutched in her hands, the glossy image of a charming front porch staring back at her. Could this be it? Her home? The thought sent a shiver down her spine, not from the coolness in the air but from the weight of it all.

She spent her childhood moving from house to house, never truly settling. She promised herself she wouldn't do the same as an adult. She vowed to create a more stable life for herself. But was she really ready to purchase her first house? A move that felt kind of permanent.

The door to *The Authenticitea Café* opened with a soft chime as Lily stepped inside, the scent of warm chai and vanilla wrapping around her. She scanned the room and spotted her real estate agent, Meghan, who looked like she was ready to give birth to her twins any moment now, already seated near the window, flipping through a stack of papers while rubbing her belly. Lily took a deep breath and joined her, placing the brochure on the table between them.

Meghan looked up with an easy smile. "You look like you've got a lot on your mind."

Lily let out a small laugh, but it was tight, uneasy. "You could say that."

She slid the stack of papers aside and leaned in slightly. "Talk to me. What's making you hesitate?"

She delayed, fingers tracing the edge of the brochure. "It's beautiful. Everything I wanted… but I'd be lying if I said I wasn't scared."

"That's normal," Meghan reassured her. "Buying your first home is a big step. But something tells me this isn't just about square footage and mortgage rates."

She exhaled slowly, then met her eyes. "I moved around a lot as a kid. Every year or two, a new house, a new school, a new life. At first, it was hard, always leaving friends behind, always being the new kid. But I figured out how to make it work."

Meghan nodded. "How so?"

"My room," she said, a small smile forming. "No matter where we moved, that was the one thing I had control over. Every house was just a structure, but my room. That was my blank canvas. I'd spend hours arranging things. Stuffed animals lined up just right, furniture shifted and reshuffled until everything felt like me."

She ran a hand over the glossy image, lost in the memory. "For my twelfth birthday, my parents finally let me decorate it exactly how I wanted. I picked the perfect color, strung up fairy lights, and got bedding that felt just right. It was the first time I felt like I had truly created a space for myself."

Her voice softened. "And then we had to move."

Meghan was quiet, listening.

"That was the hardest part, saying goodbye to something I had made my own. But I learned something. Every move, every new house, I figured out how to start over. I couldn't control where we lived, but I could control how I made it feel like home."

She paused, staring down at the brochure. "But buying a home? That's different. I never thought I'd be able to. Going down a similar path as my parents, I graduated college with not-so-great credit. For years, I assumed homeownership was something other people did—not me."

Meghan leaned back, nodding. "But you made it happen."

Lily swallowed, a mixture of nerves and pride settling in her chest. "Yeah. I worked hard to get here. Fixed my credit, saved more than I thought possible, learned everything I could about the process. I did everything right, but I'm still scared. What if something happens? What if I can't keep up?"

A gentle clink of ceramic pulled her from her thoughts. The Barista had placed a cup in front of her, a fragrant blend of cinnamon, cardamom, and vanilla. Next to it, a folded napkin.

"Right on time," Lily and Meghan said in unison, giggling as they realized what they had done.

"Jinx," Meghan said with a smirk.

Lily smiled softly, ready to see what words of wisdom would be shared today.

She ran her fingers over the words, nostalgia blooming in her chest.

Meghan tapped the brochure. "You know, you're not that kid anymore. You're not at the mercy of your parents' decisions. You've learned how to make a space feel like home no matter where you go. And this time? You're choosing this home. You're preparing for it. You're ready."

Lily swallowed, letting her words sink in. Maybe she didn't need to be afraid of making the wrong choice. Maybe, for the first time, she wasn't just chasing home, she was creating it on her own terms.

She picked up the real estate brochure, smoothing it out against the table. The house she had just toured stared back at her, its wraparound porch, its cozy fireplace.

Meghan watched her, waiting, patient. "What are you thinking?"

She met her gaze. "That maybe I don't need to be afraid anymore."

Meghan grinned. "Sounds like you already know what you want."

She exhaled, the tension in her shoulders loosening. "I think I do."

She smiled, tucking the napkin into her bag like a keepsake. Then she met Meghan's gaze, confidence settling in her chest.

Meghan glanced at the brochure. "If you decide to move forward, you know we'll need to schedule filming pretty soon. HGTV doesn't wait around."

Lily raised an eyebrow. "You're still serious about that?"

"Absolutely," Meghan grinned. "You've got the story *and* the porch. It's a perfect fit."

Lily laughed, shaking her head while taking a slow sip of the tea.

Fifteen months later, Lily sat in her living room, surrounded by friends, laughter echoing through the space.

Just as the episode was about to start, a quick knock sounded at the door. Meghan hurried in, slightly out of breath, her bag slung over her shoulder. "Sorry, sorry! Had to get the twins settled before I could leave the house. You know how it is, one needed a diaper change, the other was clinging to me for dear life."

Lily grinned, waving her inside. "No worries, you made it just in time." Meghan plopped down onto the couch with a sigh, grabbing a cup of tea from the coffee table.

She glanced at Lily with a smirk. "Look at you, a homeowner! And to think, you almost chickened out on me in that café."

Lily laughed, shaking her head. "I know, right? Good thing I had you to push me through it." "Let's do this." They were all gathered around the TV, watching the premiere of her *House Hunters* episode.

The screen showed her walking through the house, the same one she now sat in, pointing out the natural light she had fallen in love with, the cozy layout that had felt right from the start. Then, the scene cut to a familiar spot, the warm, inviting space of *The Authenticitea Café.*

On-screen, Lily sat at her favorite table, a cup of tea in her hands, deep in thought. "This café has always been a place of reflection for me," her voice played through the speakers.

"So you've made your decision?" Meghan asked her.

"Yes," Lily said, smiling from ear to ear. "I've made my decision, I'm going with—House #3."

Her friends cheered as the episode continued, showing her moving into the space, making it her own. She looked around the room, at the framed photos on the walls, the books stacked neatly on the coffee table, and the small note tucked into the corner of a picture frame the napkin from *The Authenticitea Café*, its ink slightly faded but still clear:

Stepping forward into something new will always be scary. But standing still when you're ready to grow? That's even scarier.

The smell of chai and vanilla lingered from the tea she had just brewed. This wasn't just a house. It was her home.

Lifting her cup to her lips, she took a slow, satisfying sip.

And for the first time in a long time, she felt completely at ease.

She had made the right choice. And it felt pretty darn good.

A Taste of Transitions

Change feels less like leaving and more like returning

— Inspired by Rooibos, Cinnamon, Cardamom & Vanilla —

Mood Pairing: For when you're moving through a shift; gently, bravely, and with more presence than panic.

Steep Time: Let it steep deeply. Change needs time to integrate, not just happen.

Body: Warming and grounding. Spiced with heart, softened with sweetness.

Origin: Brewed in return. Best sipped when you're navigating transformation with tenderness.

Color and Clarity

Deep amber, like firelight in a quiet room. Bold but not brash, inviting and reflective.

What part of you is returning, even as everything else evolves?

____

____

____

Aroma

Cinnamon leads with familiarity, cardamom follows with curiosity, and vanilla closes with comfort. It smells like evolution wrapped in ease.

What scent reminds you of who you've always been, even when you're becoming more?

____

____

____

Flavor

Rich and spiced, with a smooth finish. A blend that says: this is new *and* this is you.

What's changing for you—and what's staying rooted through the change?

____

____

____

Fill in the blank: I am changing, yes, but I am still ________________.

Aftertaste

A grounded sweetness that remains long after the sip. Reassurance without resistance.

What if this change isn't about fixing anything, but realigning everything?

____

____

____

Affirmation: I embrace the shift and honor the root. Change brings me home.

A Fresh Pour: Between Healing & Fulfillment

From release to presence, healing clears space for something richer. With a fresh pour, we embrace the fullness of where we are, knowing we have everything we need within us.

A Cup of Fulfillment

Leaning into bold presence, authenticity, and joy

SIP 30: A CUP OF STORM

-Dr. Taylor-

She clenched the plastic badge between her fingers, tracing the raised edges of her name as if it might anchor her. *Dr. Taylor.* It didn't feel like her name anymore. It felt like a title given to someone stronger, someone more sure of herself. Someone she wasn't sure she could be.

Dr. Taylor sat at the corner table of the café, fingers wrapped around her school ID badge as if it could hold her together. This week had unraveled her in ways she hadn't expected.

Flipped desks. Screaming students. Fights breaking out. And then, the moment that had nearly broken her—a student, no older than ten, locking eyes with her, defiant and wounded, before spitting right in her face.

She had trained for this. Studied child psychology, behavior management, de-escalation strategies. She knew her students had challenges: learning differences, trauma, emotional triggers. But the intensity of it all? No one had prepared her for that.

By Wednesday, she had spent the end of the work day in her car, the doors locked, radio off, letting silent tears trace their way down her face.

"What am I doing?" she whispered to no one.

And yet, the next morning, she walked back into the classroom.

That's why she was here now allowing herself one quiet moment, one deep breath, one sip of something warm before stepping back into the storm.

As if sensing her exhaustion, The Barista appeared, setting down a cup of dark honey-colored tea. The scent of roasted barley and cacao curled in the air—deep, earthy, with just a whisper of bitter comfort.

"Mugicha," they said, sliding it toward her. "Barley tea. Strong, grounding. Just like you."

Dr. Taylor let out a soft, tired laugh. "I don't feel very strong right now."

The Barista tilted their head, studying her. "That's usually how strength feels in the moment, messy, exhausting, like you're barely holding it together. But you keep showing up, don't you?"

They placed a neatly folded napkin beside the cup. A single sentence, handwritten in careful script:

Dr. Taylor ran her fingers over the napkin, as if pressing the words into her skin.

She took a slow sip of the tea. It was bitter, bold, grounding. The warmth settled deep inside her, filling spaces she hadn't realized were hollow.

No one had prepared her for this.

Every day felt like a battle, one where she barely had time to breathe, let alone teach. Desks flipped, chairs thrown, screams that echoed long after the room had emptied. One student had clung to her arm, sobbing uncontrollably, while another had stormed out without looking back.

Somewhere between the meltdowns and the mediation, she had begun to wonder if she was truly making a difference. If she had anything left to give.

A few weeks later, something shifted.

She had been guiding a lesson when she caught movement out of the corner of her eye—one of her most challenging students, the one who spent most of class flipping his chair or throwing pencils, watching her. Really watching.

For the first time, he wasn't trying to disrupt or escape. He was listening.

And then, just before dismissal, he hesitated at her desk, shoulders tense. Without a word, he slid a folded paper toward her and bolted for the door.

Dr. Taylor stared at it, unsure what to expect. A crude drawing? A joke at her expense?

She unfolded it carefully, her breath catching in her throat.

A rough, childlike sketch.

Scrawled in uneven letters:

"Dr. Taylor, you is nice."

Her fingers trembled as she traced the words, the lump in her throat impossible to swallow.

Maybe this was what impact looked like.

Not grand breakthroughs. Not immediate change.

But the smallest moments of connection.

The quiet proof that showing up still mattered.

Even when it felt like she wasn't making a difference at all.

She folded the note carefully, tucking it into her bag.

Tomorrow, she would show up again.

Because sometimes, strength wasn't about winning the battle.

It was simply about staying in the ring.

A Taste of Something Brewing

When you're in the thick of it

— Inspired by Mugicha (Roasted Barley Tea) —

Mood Pairing: For when you're in the middle of something big; emotionally, energetically, or spiritually and seeking strength that doesn't flinch.

Steep Time: Roast it bold. Steep it deep. Let it remind you that resilience is slow brewed.

Body: Toasty, rich, and earthy. No sweetness, just substance.

Origin: Brewed in upheaval. Best sipped when you're weathering your own inner forecast.

Color and Clarity

Dark amber, like wet earth after rain. Opaque, but steady. Clarity doesn't always come before courage.

What storm are you learning to stand in—not to be consumed by it, but to understand yourself better within it?

____

____

____

Aroma

The scent is toasted, almost smoky. It smells like strength forged through fire, not flair.

What does resilience smell like in your life—what sensory anchors ground you when everything else is shifting?

___

___

___

Flavor

Deep and roasted. No frills. Just truth. A sip that doesn't soften, it steadies.

Where in your life are you holding steady through tension, not because it's easy, but because it matters?

___

___

___

Fill in the blank: Even in the storm, I remain ______________________.

Aftertaste

Boldness that lingers. Not sharp, but undeniably present. The kind of flavor that tells you: you've made it through before, and you will again.

What strength have you discovered in the middle of the mess—not after it cleared, but while it brewed?

___

___

___

Affirmation: I sip with steadiness. I can weather what comes.

SIP 31: SAVORING LIFE'S BREW

-Aaron-

A horn blared. Aaron flinched. His breath hitched for just a second, so small that most people wouldn't notice. But he felt it. The way his chest tightened, how his fingers twitched at his side.

The car that honked wasn't even close, but the sound still sent a ripple through him, dragging him back to that night.

The crunch of metal.
The screech of tires.
The jolt, so violent it left his ears ringing.
Then, stillness.

He exhaled sharply, pressing a hand against his chest like he could smooth the tension away. His fingers brushed against the fading bruise near his collarbone, the last visible mark of his injuries. It had deepened to a shade darker than skin before softening to a dull yellow. Almost gone now. Almost.

The door to *The Authenticitea Café* jingled softly as he stepped inside. The scent of steeping herbs wrapped around him, warm and grounding, pulling him out of his thoughts like a gentle nudge. He rolled his shoulders, shaking off the stiffness.

He hadn't been here in months.

Sliding into a corner seat, Aaron rubbed the back of his neck. His hand drifted to the faint scar near his temple, a habit he hadn't shaken since the accident. His body remembered even when his mind tried to forget.

The Barista appeared with a welcoming smile, setting down a steaming cup in front of him and, as always, a folded napkin.

Aaron smirked, shaking his head. "You really never run out of these, huh?"

"Endless supply." The Barista tapped the napkin. "Go on, I know you're dying to see the wisdom in writing."

Aaron chuckled under his breath, unfolding the note.

He let out a dry laugh, shaking his head. "You do this on purpose, don't you?"

The Barista grinned. "I have *no* idea what you're talking about."

Aaron lifted his tea to his lips, inhaling the scent. "Chamomile and orange peel?"

"And a hint of cinnamon," The Barista added. "For grounding."

Aaron nodded, fingers tightening around the ceramic cup. Grounding. Yeah. He could use that. His mind drifted back—

The spinning world. The shattered glass. The eerie silence that followed.

"I didn't even see it coming," he murmured, more to himself than to The Barista. "One second, I was just driving, thinking about nothing in particular. Then—" He snapped his fingers. "Everything changed."

The Barista eyes steady on him without interrupting.

"They kept calling me *lucky*," Aaron said, tapping a finger against the table. "Like I should be grateful. And, I mean, I *am*—" He exhaled through his nose. "But it wasn't luck that stuck with me. It was the reminder of how fragile it all is. How one moment can change everything."

The Barista nodded slowly. "So, naturally, you spent months spiraling in existential dread."

Aaron let out a short laugh, shaking his head. "Yeah, pretty much."

"And now?"

He hesitated, then smiled. "Now… I just laugh at it."

The Barista raised an eyebrow. "At *the accident*?"

"No, at soup."

"…Soup."

Aaron chuckled. "I had my arm in a cast, trying to eat soup one night. Spilled half of it all over myself. I looked so ridiculous, just this grown man, covered in soup, that I lost it. I started laughing, and I couldn't stop." He shook his head, amused at the memory. "And I realized, this whole time, I'd been gripping fear so tightly that I forgot how to live."

He met The Barista's gaze, lifting his cup. "I could've died that night. But I didn't. So, if I'm here, I might as well enjoy it. Find reasons to laugh. To *feel*. To live."

The Barista leaned back. "Sounds like a good reason to steep in the moment."

Aaron raised his cup in agreement, the scent of orange and cinnamon rising with the steam.

"Yeah," he said, taking a sip. "I think so too."

A Sip of Everyday Light

Notice the everyday

— Inspired by Herbal Tisane —

Mood Pairing: For when you want to pause, not to rest from life, but to steep more fully in it.

Steep Time: Let it steep like a golden hour, unrushed, glowing, fleeting in the best way.

Body: Smooth, mellow, and fragrant. The kind of blend that makes you slow your sip.

Origin: Brewed in presence. Best sipped when life feels full, and you want to feel it more.

Color and Clarity

Warm amber with golden edges. Like sunlight captured in a cup. It's not about clarity, it's about glow.

Where in your life are you being invited to slow down and savor?

____

____

____

Aroma

Fragrant and soothing. A delicate harmony of earthy and floral, with hints of sweetness beneath. It smells like comfort and celebration in the same breath.

What does gratitude smell like to you? What scent brings you back to joy?

____

____

____

Flavor

Full-bodied without heaviness. A sip that doesn't rush, it rolls. It tastes like presence, like "right now" in liquid form.

Where have you been so focused on progress that you've missed the pleasure of being here?

____

____

____

Fill in the blank: I give myself permission to savor __________________.

Aftertaste

A lingering warmth that reminds you: this moment matters, too. Not because it's big, but because it's *yours.*

What's something small that deserves your full attention today?

____

____

____

Affirmation: I sip slowly. I savor deeply. This is enough.

SIP 32: A SPOONFUL OF LAUGHTER

-Kim-

Not every stand-up set begins with the scent of chai, but then again, not every comic starts in a tea café.

Kim scanned the room, eyeing the audience with their porcelain teacups as she adjusted the mic stand with a playful shake.

"Alright," she said, a smile tugging at the corner of her mouth, "We're almost ready. Not every day you get to do stand-up in a tea café."

She glanced around the room, then back at the mic.

"I told my cousin I was performing here, and he goes, 'Cool. Do they serve wine?' I said, 'Nope, but if you steep that chamomile long enough, you might forget your problems just the same.'"

A ripple of laughter moved through the room.

She grinned, warming up.

"Seriously though, nothing keeps you grounded like trying to be funny while someone next to you is ordering a lavender oat milk latte with extra froth… and a side of emotional healing."

This time, the laughter grew, richer, more relaxed. The kind that told her the room was with her.

She gave a playful bow of her head, then stepped back from the mic. The soft spotlight followed her as she made her way to the counter. The Barista, already in sync with her rhythm, slid a warm cup of tea her way. A small, folded note leaned against the rim—a ritual that never failed to make her smile.

Kim picked it up, unfolding the delicate paper with steady fingers.

She exhaled, her smirk softening into something deeper.

She glanced at her tea, chai. Spiced, bold, full of warmth. Fitting. She took a sip, letting the flavors bloom on her tongue, each note layered like a well-crafted joke.

Comedy had always been her way of making sense of things. A way to turn discomfort into connection, to take the awkward, the painful, the downright ridiculous, and spin it into something that made people lean in rather than turn away. But it hadn't always been easy.

She had been the kid who asked too many questions, the one teachers either adored or barely tolerated. The one who got in trouble for talking too much, for laughing when no one else thought it was funny, for turning serious moments into something lighter. For years, she had struggled, trying to fit into a world that didn't seem to have a space for her brand of humor and curiosity.

your light is meant to stand out.

The words tugged at something deep inside her, pulling her back to a third-grade multiplication contest.

She could still feel the rough fabric of the stuffed Rudolph the Red-Nosed Reindeer in her hands, the prize she had won after weeks of drilling times tables she swore she'd never use in real life. It wasn't about the contest. It wasn't even about the prize. It was about *being seen*, about the realization that, like Rudolph, the very thing that had made her different, the thing she had been teased for, was also one of her greatest strengths.

She hadn't made the connection at the time, but there had to be a reason she held onto that stuffed reindeer for all these years. Something in her had known.

Still, if she was being honest, the real turning point didn't come until later.

She had met Lori in a community college speech class, a required course she had been dreading. The idea of preparing structured speeches made her stomach churn. She could riff, she could improvise, but crafting a formal talk? That felt like an impossible ask.

Lori had been different from anyone Kim had ever met, self-assured, deeply introspective, the kind of person who didn't just *speak* but *made people listen.* And yet, she had a quiet way of encouraging others, making them feel seen in a way Kim had never experienced before.

When it was Kim's turn to present, she had frozen in front of the class, blanking on her carefully written speech about *the psychology of laughter.* The silence stretched. Her palms were clammy. She could hear someone shifting in their seat, waiting.

And then, Lori.

From the front row, she had simply smiled, raised her eyebrows, and whispered, *"Just make us laugh."*

That was all Kim needed.

She threw the speech out the window (figuratively, of course) and just *talked.* About how she had once laughed so hard in church she snorted in the middle of a sermon. About how humor had been the only thing that got her through her parents' divorce. About how sometimes, a well-placed joke was the difference between connection and isolation.

By the time she finished, the class was wiping tears from their eyes, some from laughter, some from something deeper.

And she knew.

This was it.

Lori had seen something in her before she had seen it in herself. That day, over bad cafeteria coffee, Lori had looked at her and said, *"You know you could actually do this, right? Like… for real?"*

Kim had laughed, shaking her head. "Stand-up? No way."

But the idea stuck.

It was Lori who encouraged her to go to her first open mic. Lori who helped her refine her stories. Lori who, even now, was probably sitting somewhere in the audience, waiting for her to own her space.

She stirred her tea, watching the swirl of spices settle, just as she had learned to settle into her own skin.

A voice called out, "You ready, Kim?"

She grinned, grabbing the mic.

"Born ready."

As the first wave of laughter rippled through the room, she knew one thing for sure:

This time, she wasn't dimming her light for anyone.

A Taste of Whimsi-Tea

Lighten the mood

— Inspired by Masala Chai with a Citrus Twist —

Mood Pairing: For when you need a good laugh, a strong brew, and a reminder not to take it *all* so seriously.

Steep Time: Brew with boldness. Let the flavors mingle like stories told around a table.

Body: Strong, spicy, and full of character, just like your favorite comedian..

Origin: Brewed in resilience and play. Best sipped when you need a little levity to balance the heaviness.

Color and Clarity

Deep brown with a golden hue, like a chai latte kissed by sunshine. Comforting, familiar, with just enough twist to keep it interesting.

When was the last time you let yourself laugh out loud—not as a distraction, but as a release?

____

____

____

Aroma

Bold spices, cardamom, clove, cinnamon, meet a surprise zest of citrus. It smells like a punchline just waiting to be delivered.

What scents bring a smile to your face before you even sip?

____

____

____

Flavor

Spicy and warm, with a tangy sparkle. A brew that makes you raise an eyebrow *and* your spirits.

Where could a little humor shift your perspective today?

____

____

____

Fill in the blank: I'm learning to laugh even when ________.

Aftertaste

Lingering spice with a citrus lift. It reminds you that joy doesn't cancel depth, it colors it.

What's a moment of laughter you want to carry with you longer?

____

____

____

Affirmation: I welcome laughter into my healing. I steep joy into my day, one sip at a time.

SIP 33: A PERFECTLY IMPERFECT POUR

-Jay and Vi-

Vi adjusted her scarf with the same motion she'd used for decades, tug, twist, tuck, muscle memory rooted in seasons past. But today, it wasn't about the cold.

The door of *The Authenticitea Café* creaked open as Vi and Jay stepped inside, bringing a whisper of the evening's chill with them. Vi paused at the threshold. Forty-two years of love, and somehow this moment still felt as fragile as their first date. Jay placed a reassuring hand at the small of her back, gently guiding her to their favorite table tucked near the window.

This was their spot, a quiet corner where countless conversations had unfolded. Not every week, not always together, but often enough to feel like a place where their stories were welcomed without expectation.

Vi settled into her chair with a soft sigh, her eyes brightening as Jay tucked the chair in behind her.

"You know I can manage," she teased, adjusting her scarf.

"I know," Jay replied, his voice warm and familiar, "but let an old man feel useful every once in a while."

She smiled, reaching across the table for his hand. Their fingers intertwined easily, a practiced dance refined over their years together.

Four decades of quiet mornings, unexpected challenges, joyful discoveries, and the subtle sweetness of knowing someone deeply and being known in return.

Just then, a burst of laughter caught their attention. A young family at the nearby table was navigating the joyful chaos of small children, one toddler dropped a spoon loudly onto the floor while his sister giggled at the commotion. The parents exchanged patient, amused glances as the father bent to retrieve the fallen utensil.

Vi watched the family warmly, her eyes twinkling. The little girl, noticing Vi's gaze, shyly waved, prompting Vi to wave back gently, a soft laugh escaping her lips.

"Remember those days?" Vi asked Jay softly, nostalgia coloring her voice.

Jay chuckled quietly. "I do. Though I can't say I miss the constant chasing around."

Vi's expression grew thoughtful. "I just don't want to become a burden to our kids, you know? They're busy with their own lives, their own families."

Jay nodded slowly, his gaze tender yet understanding. "I know, Vi. And they're good kids, they'd do anything we asked. But it's hard, isn't it? Asking for help when we spent so long being the ones offering it."

She sighed softly. "Health isn't getting easier, and the finances… well, they stretch a bit thinner each year."

Jay squeezed her hand gently. "We'll manage, just as we always have. Together."

The Barista approached, placing their cups gently before them with a warm smile. "Tonight's blend is elderberry for strength, lavender for peace, and honey, because every moment deserves a touch of sweetness."

Jay raised his cup slightly in gratitude. "Perfect timing."

Vi cupped the tea in her hands, breathing in deeply, savoring the comforting aroma. "Feels like exactly what we need."

The Barista set a folded napkin between them and quietly moved away, allowing them their privacy.

Jay unfolded the napkin, reading the handwritten note softly:

Vi's eyes softened as she reflected on the words. "Do you ever wonder if we could've done things differently?"

Jay looked thoughtfully at their intertwined hands resting on the table. "Of course. But every choice led us here, didn't it? To this moment, together."

Her gaze drifted toward the window, watching the quiet rhythm of life outside, the hopeful laughter of young families, couples sharing secrets, the world moving gently forward. She squeezed Jay's hand softly. "I suppose we did find our own way, didn't we?"

Jay nodded, his eyes gentle and full of certainty. "Our way wasn't perfect. But it was ours, Vi. And that's exactly how it was meant to be."

As they sipped their tea, the young mother from the nearby table stood briefly, scooping the toddler into her arms. She caught Vi's eye and shared a knowing smile, a silent acknowledgment passing between them, the understanding that life, in all its chaos and calm, was a blend worth savoring.

In the gentle glow of lamplight, Vi lifted her tea once more, savoring the warmth that filled her cup and her heart. Jay mirrored her, each sip an acknowledgment of the years behind them and the quiet strength they'd found in choosing each other, again and again.

A Taste of Enoughness

The space between effort and ease

— Inspired by Elderberry, Lavender & Honeybush Herbal Blend —

Mood Pairing: For when things aren't going exactly right, but somehow, feel right enough.

Steep Time: Let it steep without pressure. The best pours are often the ones that spill a little.

Body: Smooth, mellow, and slightly floral with an earthy grounding.

Origin: Brewed in acceptance. Best sipped when you need to remember that wholeness can be messy.

Color and Clarity

A dusky plum hue, like twilight settling after a long day. Not bright. Not clear. Still, beautiful.

Where in your life are you learning to love what's unfolding, even if it's not what you planned?

____

____

____

Aroma

Lavender leads, with honeybush weaving in sweetness and elderberry grounding it all. It smells like resolution without resistance.

What does your version of "peaceful enough" smell like? Feel like?

____

____

____

Flavor

Soft and steady. Slightly tart from elderberry, rounded by floral calm. A blend that doesn't perform—it simply *is*.

Where could you release the pressure to "get it right" and instead honor what's real?

____

____

____

Fill in the blank: I don't have to be perfect to feel ________________.

Aftertaste

A lingering calm that reminds you: you've come far enough to rest here. No need to fix, just be.

What imperfections are becoming part of your story in the best way?

____

____

____

Affirmation: I honor what's whole and what's healing. I sip peace in all its forms.

SIP 34: THE BREW THAT YOU CHOSE

-Erica-

Erica reached for her tea, expecting the napkin to be there, the one that always held more than just words. But today, the table was bare.

She curled her hands around the delicate porcelain cup, letting the scent of jasmine green tea wrap around her. Cinnamon and cardamom lingered in the air, mingling with the floral steam as she watched the soft swirl of liquid inside.

It reminded her of *the* dress, deep, rich, unexpected.

She exhaled slowly, taking a sip, waiting for the familiar moment that came with every visit. A small pause. A message written just for her.

Her fingers brushed the smooth wooden table again, then paused. She glanced down at the floor, wondering if maybe she had dropped it. But there was nothing there, only the steady hum of conversation and the quiet clink of teacups.

The absence pulsed louder now.

Every time she came in, The Barista gave her a small, folded piece of paper with a handwritten message, sometimes an affirmation, sometimes a question that lingered long after she left. It had become part of her ritual.

She glanced toward the counter, catching The Barista's eye. "Did you forget about me today?" she teased.

The Barista's lips curled into a knowing smile as she shook her head. "Not at all. I just figured you'd want it when the moment was right."

Erica blinked, curiosity flickering in her chest, but before she could press further, Julia slid into the seat across from her, her coat still draped over her shoulders.

"Okay, tell me again why we're canceling this appointment," Julia said, flipping through her planner. "I *blocked off* this afternoon to go wedding dress shopping, Erica. I even mentally prepared for those weird corset contraptions."

Rachel slid in beside her, raising an eyebrow. "Yeah, this better be good."

Sophia, the last to arrive, settled in with a calm smile. "I have a feeling it is."

Erica grinned, wrapping her hands around her tea. "It is. Because I already found my dress."

Julia's planner hit the table with a *thwap.* "Excuse me?"

Rachel's eyes narrowed playfully. "You went *without us?*"

"Not intentionally!" Erica laughed. "It just… happened. I stopped by this boutique on a whim, and the moment I tried it on, I *knew.*"

Sophia leaned forward, resting her chin on her hand. "Okay, I need details. What kind of dress are we talking?"

Erica hesitated, fingers drifting to the necklace at her collarbone. "Before I tell you that, let me tell you about *this* first."

She unclasped it, laying it gently on the wooden table, watching as the tiny Swarovski flowers and delicate green leaves caught the café's soft light.

Rachel leaned in first. "Wait. I don't think I've ever really looked at this up close."

Sophia smiled knowingly. "I have."

Julia picked it up carefully, tilting it toward the light. "It's beautiful. What's the story?"

Erica let the warmth of her tea settle her before she spoke.

"I used to stare at this necklace for hours when I was a kid," she said softly. "It sat in my mom's curio cabinet, behind glass, like a museum piece. I never touched it, I didn't even *think* to. It was too special. Too *not mine.*"

She paused, watching the necklace shimmer as Julia set it back down.

"My great-grandmother, Linda, bought it decades ago. She wasn't even planning to, her sister-in-law admired it first, then changed her mind. My great-grandmother took one look and said, *If you're not going to buy it, I am.* And that was that. But she never really *wore* it. My mom inherited it later, and it still sat behind glass.

Then, recently, my mom handed me a small box." Erica's voice softened. "And I *knew* before I even opened it."

Rachel's eyes softened. "It was yours."

Erica nodded. "I always thought I'd just get to borrow it one day. But then, suddenly, it *was* mine. And I knew, right then, it had to be part of my wedding."

She glanced down at it again, tracing her fingers over the crystals. "I thought I'd just pair it with a white dress and be done with it. But something about that felt… off. The necklace didn't *feel like it belonged* with white dress. It should be paired with something…well, different."

She took a deep breath, looking up at them.

"And then, the boutique owner pulled out *the dress.*"

She let the words linger before adding, "Velvet."

A beat of silence.

Julia's slapped her hands on the tables. "Velvet?"

Erica smiled. "And… it's green."

Rachel blinked. "Green?"

Julia stared at her like she'd just announced she was wearing a costume instead. "You mean, like, an *actual* green dress? Not, like, a soft sage, or a tint of seafoam, or something bridal-esque?"

"Deep emerald," Erica confirmed, already bracing for their reactions.

"But—green? For a *wedding*?"

Sophia, ever the voice of quiet confidence, grinned. "I *love* this for you."

Rachel exhaled, sitting back. "Huh. Okay, I didn't see that coming."

Julia leaned forward, intrigued now. "Okay, but I need to *see* this. Please tell me you took a picture."

Erica pulled out her phone, scrolling to the image, then turned it around.

The screen glowed softly as her bridesmaids leaned in.

Sophia let out a slow, appreciative exhale. "Wow."

Julia's expression shifted as she studied it. "Okay. I see it now. The necklace *does* belong with that dress."

Rachel, the holdout, sighed. "Alright, I'm officially on board." She sat back. "But now that you're going full unconventional, what are *we* wearing?"

Erica hesitated, setting her phone down.

"Actually… I was thinking," she started carefully, "maybe we don't do bridesmaid dresses at all."

Rachel's eyebrows shot up. "I *knew* it. You're going rogue."

Erica laughed. "No, listen. I don't want you all in matching dresses that you'll never wear again. What if instead, we do a color palette? Something that lets each of you pick something that fits *you*?"

Sophia smiled. "So instead of trying to fit us into a single image, you're letting us define our own."

Erica tilted her head, considering the words. "Yeah. I guess I am."

Sophia pointing toward Erica. "I see you rewriting the rules."

Their hands met in the center, laughter spilling between them.

As they leaned back, The Barista appeared at Erica's side, slipping a folded piece of paper onto the table.

"You're ready for it now," she said softly.

Erica hesitated, then carefully unfolded the note. The inked words were simple yet profound:

She ran her fingers over the words, her throat tightening just slightly.

It wasn't just about the necklace. Or the dress. Or even what her bridesmaids would wear.

It was about claiming this moment as her own.

A Taste of Truth

How you're designed to show up

— Inspired by Jasmine Velvet Blend: Jasmine Green Tea with Cardamom & Cinnamon —

Mood Pairing: For when you're standing at a threshold, or simply remembering that you always have a say.

Steep Time: Let it bloom. Let it warm. Let it remind you that choice isn't pressure, it's power.

Body: Silky and balanced. Jasmine floats. Spices ground.

Origin: Brewed in alignment. Best sipped when you're choosing, not reacting.

Color and Clarity

Golden green with a soft shimmer, like morning light through mist. It's the color of decisions made with heart.

What choice have you made recently that honors your inner knowing?

____

____

____

Aroma

Jasmine leads with grace, cardamom and cinnamon follow with warmth.It smells like elegance with an edge.

What scent or moment reminds you that you're the one writing your story?

____

____

____

Flavor

Delicate yet confident. A layered sip that asks you to slow down and savor what's yours. It's the taste of ownership—and gentle certainty.

What would choosing yourself more often look like in small, daily ways?

____

____

____

Fill in the blank: I choose ____________________ *because it feels like* me.

Aftertaste

A quiet heat and floral linger—soft, steady, true. Not the kind of bold that shouts. The kind that doesn't need to.

What's a choice you're proud of—even if no one else sees it?

____

____

____

Affirmation: I honor my inner voice. I choose my brew—and my path—with care.

SIP 35: TRADITIONS IN EVERY SIP

-Langston-

Some absences don't echo, they settle quietly, folding themselves into familiar spaces.

As the door to the tea café chimed softly, Langston hesitated. The familiar hum of conversation wove through the air, threading itself between the clink of ceramic cups and the muted shuffle of pages turning. The scent of steeped spices curled around him, warm, grounding.

His hands remained in his pockets, fingers brushing against the worn cuff of his sweatshirt. He exhaled slowly. Grief had a way of settling in the quiet moments, in the places where memory slipped in unannounced.

At the counter, The Barista was already preparing a cup. Not out of assumption, but out of memory. A quiet kind of knowing.

Without asking, they slid a cup toward him, the deep indigo hue swirling like ink in water. A delicate citrus-floral aroma rose in soft steam, grounding and familiar. Beside it, a folded napkin. Handwritten words in smooth, familiar strokes:

Langston ran his fingers over the words, his throat tightening.

"You always knew what he needed before he even asked," he murmured, lifting his eyes to The Barista.

A small, knowing smile. "Mm".

They didn't need to say his grandfather's name. The memories were stitched into this place —in the chair near the back, in the years of quiet conversations over cups of tea. Langston and his grandfather had been coming here for as long as he could remember.

"Still wearing that sweatshirt, huh?" The Barista said, a softness in their voice.

Langston let out a chuckle, shaking his head. "Haven't washed it. And I don't plan to anytime soon."

The Barista just nodded, as if they understood completely.

His gaze drifted toward the back of the café, past the usual clusters of people deep in conversation, to the small book nook near the restroom. There it was. The old leather chair.

It had been there for years, tucked away, always a little separate from the rest—like it was waiting for someone who knew how to appreciate a quiet moment.

His grandfather used to sit there sometimes, flipping through the local paper, the deep creases in his brow smoothing as he sipped his tea. Even when he spoke, his voice carried the steady warmth of a lesson in disguise.

"It's not about where you go, Langston. It's about the pieces of yourself you leave behind."

Back then, Langston had rolled his eyes, too young to understand the weight of those words. But now, standing in this café, the air thick with memory, he felt the truth of them.

Growing up, his grandfather wasn't just a storyteller, he was the kind of man who found meaning in everything. A drive to the trash transfer station became a lesson in responsibility. The way he tied his tie, precisely, methodically, became a reminder that the smallest details mattered.

But there was one tradition that stood above the rest.

LU.

Langston University wasn't just a school to his grandfather, it was the foundation of his life. It's where he met Langston's grandmother, where their story began, and where his legacy took root. He believed in it so deeply; he convinced his son and daughter-in-law to name their firstborn grandson after the university. When he shared memories, they weren't about grades or classrooms, they were about the people, the moments, and the life lessons that stretched far beyond any textbook.

And with that passion came the LU Lions paraphernalia: sweatshirts, hats, ties, and the custom bright orange and blue blazer he wore on special occasions. Langston used to think it was just a funny piece of clothing, something too bold, too loud. But to his grandfather, it wasn't just fabric.

It was a thread in the story of his life.

Langston inherited many of those items after his grandfather passed. Some folded neatly into his collection, blending with the ones he had gathered over the years. But the ones that carried his grandfather's scent, faint, familiar, powerful, those were different.

The first time he slipped on his grandfather's sweatshirt, the scent of home, of love, of legacy wrapped around him like a quiet embrace. He closed his eyes and was right back there sitting beside his grandfather, listening, learning.

He never washed it. He didn't plan to.

Because some things shouldn't be washed away.

Now, as he sat at his usual table in the café, he found himself staring at the old leather chair again. He thought about his own children.

Would they know their great-grandfather beyond the faded photographs and the stories Langston would tell? Would they understand that legacy wasn't just about what someone left behind, it was about the way they lived on in the smallest moments?

He smiled to himself, remembering how his daughter had tugged on his sleeve just the other day, pointing to the Lions sweatshirt hanging in his closet.

"Is that Grandpa's?"

He nodded.

"Can I wear it?"

For a split second, he had hesitated. Not because he didn't want her to, but because he knew the moment she put it on, the scent would start to fade.

But then he saw the way her fingers traced the embroidered letters, the curiosity in her eyes, the quiet kind of reverence.

"Yeah," he had said, handing it over. "But only if you promise to take care of it."

She grinned. "I will."

And that's when he realized, his grandfather's legacy wasn't fading. It was being carried forward.

Langston took another slow sip of tea, watching the blue deepen with each movement of the cup, a quiet reminder that legacy shifts but never fades.

“Everything he taught me, every small moment, every lesson woven into the quietest spaces, I’m passing down,” he said, more to himself than to The Barista. “It’s in how I raise my kids, in the values I teach them. It’s in every decision I make. “The Barista gave a slow nod. “That’s how it should be.”

Langston lingered, rubbing his hands over the arm of the leather chair one last time before pushing himself up.

“Same time next week?” The Barista asked, already knowing the answer.

Langston chuckled, slipping his hands into his pockets. “Yeah. Same time next week.”

As he stepped outside, the crisp air wrapped around him, and for the first time in weeks, the weight on his shoulders felt less like grief and more like something else.

Something steady. Something unbreakable. Something stitched into time itself.

A Taste of Legacy

Carrying forward what truly matters

— Inspired by Butterfly Pea Flower & Earl Grey Twist —

Mood Pairing: For when you're honoring memory and carrying the thread forward.

Steep Time: Let it rest long enough for the color to bloom. Let memory unfold in layers.

Body: Velvety and deep. Earthy, with a quiet floral depth. Like stories that echo through generations..

Origin: Rooted in memory, carried in ritual. Best sipped when remembering where it all began.

Color and Clarity

A rich, soulful blue, quiet and bold. Legacy doesn't shout. It endures.

What tradition or memory is steeping in your heart today?

____

____

____

Aroma

Earthy, calming, touched with citrus and the scent of worn cotton. Like old photographs and familiar voices.

What scents bring you back to the roots of who you are?

____

____

____

Flavor

Gentle at first, then unexpectedly full. A blend that holds presence, just like the sweatshirt still hanging in your closet.

What do you carry that helps you remember who you are?

____

____

____

Fill in the blank: One tradition I choose to honor is ________.

Aftertaste

Subtle, but unforgettable. The kind of finish that stays with you through the next cup—and the next generation.

What tradition grounds you, no matter where you go?

____

____

____

Affirmation: I carry the stories that shaped me. I sip from legacy and pour into tomorrow.

SIP 36: STEEPING IN POSSIBILITY

-Quinton-

The bell above the café door jingled as Quinton and his dad stepped into *The Authenticitea Café*. The smell of warm cinnamon and honey igniting Quinton's sweet senses, but it did little to settle the tight knot in his stomach. He clutched his dad's hand, his other hand buried deep in his hoodie pocket.

He didn't want to be here.

He didn't want to go to his reading lesson either.

His teacher had told his parents that he might need to repeat the year, to help him get "caught up" on his reading and comprehension. The words had sat heavy in his chest, like a weight he couldn't shake. But his parents knowing their son was more than capable didn't think he needed to start over. They said he just needed a little more support.

Quinton wasn't feeling so confident.

His dad led him to a table near the window, ruffling his hair before taking a seat across from him. "Got a few minutes before we head to Miss Kay's," he said with a grin.

Miss Kay. Quinton liked her. She never made him feel slow, never sighed when he got stuck on a word. And she had a giant jar of popcorn on her desk. He got to scoop out a whole handful after every lesson—sometimes two if he worked extra hard.

But no matter how much popcorn he ate, reading still felt impossible.

"I don't think I'll ever be good at it," Quinton muttered, kicking at the chair leg.

His dad leaned forward, resting his arms on the table. "You don't have to be good at it yet," he said. "But you will be."

Quinton frowned. "How do you know?"

Before his dad could answer, The Barista appeared at their table, setting a warm vanilla rooibos tea in front of Quinton. He blinked up at them, surprised.

"Vanilla for comfort," they said, sliding a folded napkin beside the cup. "And a little extra sweetness for patience."

Quinton hesitated before unfolding the napkin.

His eyebrows scrunched as he stared at the words. The letters sat on the page, shifting in and out of focus. He recognized some of them, but the rest twisted and turned, refusing to settle into something that made sense.

His dad noticed the hesitation and scooted his chair closer. "Want to sound it out together?" he asked gently.

Quinton nodded hesitantly. His dad ran his finger under the first few words.

"Every... great... reader..."

Quinton followed his dad's voice, his lips moving along with the words.

"Was... once a... beginner."

Quinton exhaled, his shoulders dropping slightly.

"See?" His dad smiled. "One word at a time, just like the note says."

Quinton wasn't sure it was that simple. He wasn't a reader. Not really. But something about the way his dad said it—like it was already true, like it was just a matter of time, made him want to believe, even just a little bit.

He took a small sip of the tea. It was warm and smooth, like melted vanilla ice cream.

Maybe one day, he thought.

Several years later, Quinton found himself sitting at the same café, only this time, he wasn't alone for long.

A stack of books sat beside him, their covers bright and inviting. His name, printed in bold letters across the front, still felt surreal.

Quinton Smith, Children's Author.

He had been invited to lead today's children's circle time, to read aloud from his very own book.

It was still strange to think about, the fact that he could sit down and fill pages with words, that he could get lost in books for hours, that stories now felt like home rather than a locked door.

Every now and then he'd get tripped on some words reading too fast made his brain feel tangled. But he had learned to slow down, to let the words settle.

The café door chimed, and a father and his young son walked in, hand in hand. Quinton watched as they settled into the same window seat he had once sat in all those years ago. The little boy slouched in his chair, arms crossed tight, his face set in quiet frustration.

Quinton smiled. He knew that feeling well.

A moment later, The Barista arrived at their table, setting down a warm cup of vanilla rooibos in front of the boy, along with a folded napkin. The little boy hesitated, then, curiosity getting the better of him, carefully unfolded the note.

His brow furrowed as he stared at the words. Letters shifted and tangled together, just as they once had for Quinton.

And then, just like his own father had done, the boy's dad leaned in, guiding him through it—one word at a time.

Quinton didn't have to see the words to know what they said.

He had once held that very same quote in his hands.

As he turned back toward the children's circle, he heard a small voice from across the café.

"Hey, Dad?"

Quinton glanced up just in time to see the little boy tugging at his father's sleeve.

"Can we stay for the story before we go?"

His dad hesitated, checking his watch. "I don't know, buddy. We've got somewhere to be soon."

The little boy fidgeted. "Please? Just a little bit?"

Quinton smiled.

The dad exhaled, ruffling his son's hair, the same way Quinton's dad used to do. "Alright. Just a little bit."

The little boy grinned, slipping off his chair and hurrying over to the circle of kids. He plopped down on the rug, glancing up at Quinton expectantly.

Quinton picked up his book, ran his fingers over the cover, and took a deep breath.

He smiled.

"This story isn't about a hero. It's about someone who kept going," he began.

A Taste of Not yet

Trusting when the outcome remains unseen

— Inspired by Vanilla Rooibos, Honey & Chamomile —

Mood Pairing: For when you're not sure what's next, but want to believe in what could be.

Steep Time: Let it steep long. Possibility asks for patience, not pressure.

Body: Smooth and nurturing. Gentle enough to soften doubt.

Origin: Brewed in hope. Best sipped when you're waiting, wondering, or dreaming again.

Color and Clarity

A warm, amber hue with golden undertones. Not quite clear, just like the future. But warm, nonetheless.

What are you quietly nurturing right now, even if no one else can see it yet?

____

____

____

Aroma

Vanilla and honey rise first, sweet and soothing. Chamomile follows like a whisper. It smells like trust in progress, not perfection.

What does possibility smell like to you today?

____

____

____

Flavor

Soft, mellow, and slow to unfold. Each sip builds comfort, like a gentle reminder that you're not behind. It's a flavor that says, *you don't need the answer, just the next step.*

Where might you offer yourself more patience as something new brews within or around you?

____

____

____

Fill in the blank: I am steeping ____________________ into being.

Aftertaste

A gentle sweetness with lingering calm. It reminds you that some things don't arrive fast, but they *do* arrive.

What vision are you holding onto, even if it's still steeping?

____

____

____

Affirmation: I honor the in-between. I steep gently. I grow with grace.

SIP 37: A CUP OF STRENGTH

-Alexis-

The storm outside had rolled in fast, drenching the city in sheets of relentless rain. Thunder grumbled in the distance, and the wind howled through the alleyways, rattling the windows of the café. Every time the door opened, another soaked customer rushed inside, shaking out their umbrella, exhaling relief.

But Alexis barely noticed any of it.

She sat at the corner booth, her fingers wrapped around a cup of chai, the warmth doing little to steady the simmering frustration inside her. The seat across from her was empty, for now. But she knew they'd come. She had called them, voice tight with something raw, something pressing.

And they had answered.

The bell over the door jingled, and a rush of cool air blew in as Michelle and Jada stepped inside, their coats soaked, their faces filled with concern.

"Girl, I got your text, what happened?" Michelle asked, shaking water from her arms as she slid into the booth across from Alexis.

"Are you okay?" Jada added, shrugging out of her jacket, squeezing Alexis's wrist before sitting down.

Alexis let out a long breath. Now that they were here, the words lodged in her throat, tangled between frustration and exhaustion.

She stared at the ripples in her tea before finally speaking. "It happened again."

Jada didn't need clarification. "Damn," she muttered.

Michelle exhaled sharply. "When?"

"Earlier. I was just walking. Minding my business. And out of nowhere, some guy drives past, rolls down his window, and yells, the N-word" Her voice caught for a second. She forced herself to keep going. "Yells at me like I don't belong here. Like I don't have the right to exist in this space."

Jada's jaw clenched. Michelle shook her head, muttering something under her breath.

The café hummed with quiet conversation, the hiss of steaming milk, the clinking of ceramic cups. Outside, lightning split the sky, casting a brief glow against the rain-streaked windows.

"I don't get it," Alexis continued, her voice quieter now, heavier. "Our people have come so far. And yet, here we are. Still having to deal with this blatant hatred like we're stuck in some twisted loop."

Jada scoffed. "Like our grandparents didn't already fight this fight. Like our parents didn't push back against the same ignorance."

"It's exhausting," Michelle said, rubbing her temples. "I swear, the way people act, like we should just 'get over it'—meanwhile, we're still *living* it."

"Exactly." Alexis exhaled sharply, shaking her head. "And the worst part? It still *stings*. I still feel it, deep in my bones, like I'm back in middle school all over again."

Jada leaned in. "Middle school?"

Alexis hesitated, then let herself go there.

"Yeah", she said with a puff of air. I was twelve," she said, her voice distant, as if pulling the memory from a place she didn't visit often. "There was this boy. He liked me, I *knew* he did. The way he looked at me, the way he always found a reason to talk to me. And I liked him too. Then one day, he just… stopped."

She could still see his face, the way he avoided her gaze, the way his voice had wavered when he finally spoke.

"We can't talk anymore." "Why?" "My parents said I will never be allowed to date a Black girl."

A pause settled between them.

Jada shook her head, arms crossed. "God. That never really leaves you, does it?"

"No," Alexis admitted. "It doesn't."

They sat in silence for a moment, listening to the rain beat against the windows, letting the weight of it all settle between them.

Then, movement at the edge of the table.

The Barista approached first, carrying a small clay teapot and three ceramic cups. Their expression was unreadable, but their movements were deliberate, precise. Without a word, they poured the tea, steam curling into the air, the scent of earth and spice filling the space between them.

Beside them, an older woman, wrapped in a deep navy shawl, smiled warmly.

"A stormy night deserves a strong tea," she said, watching The Barista's careful movements.

Jada frowned. "Did we order this?"

The woman shook her head. "No. But it was needed."

She thanked The Barista as they placed the last cup on the table and slid a folded napkin beside Alexis's hand. The Barista didn't linger. No explanations, no words. Just a glance—brief, knowing—before they disappeared behind the counter.

The older woman stayed a moment longer. "It's rooibos," she said, nodding toward the tea. "A tea from South Africa. My grandmother used to make it when the world felt too heavy."

Jada lifted the cup first, inhaling. "Smells like… the earth after it rains."

The woman nodded. "It grows in dry, unforgiving soil. But it thrives anyway." She turned slightly toward Alexis then followed her glance to others, her expression gentle. "And so will you."

Alexis swallowed, fingers tightening around the cup.

Then, she glanced down noticing the napkin, with interest she picked up and read.

Jada and Michelle leaned in.

"Damn," Jada whispered.

Michelle let out a breathy laugh. "The universe really said, 'You needed to hear this tonight.'"

Alexis picked up her cup, letting the warmth spread through her fingers, through her chest.

She wasn't that little girl anymore.

She would never let the world make her feel small again.

And like the rooibos, she would thrive.

A Taste of Self-worth

Reclaiming your light

— *Inspired by Stormbrew: Rooibos, Cinnamon & Cacao Nibs* —

Mood Pairing: For when you're weathering something hard, and finding your footing anyway.

Steep Time: Strong and slow. Let the heat build. Let the strength rise.

Body: Full-bodied, earthy, with a warming bite. This one doesn't whisper, it hums with quiet power.

Origin: Brewed in challenge. Best sipped when you're rebuilding, re-centering, or simply refusing to give up.

Color and Clarity

A deep, rust-red brew that looks like it's been through fire, and came out richer for it. There's clarity in the complexity.

What part of your strength has surprised you lately?

____

____

____

Aroma

Cinnamon heat, grounding rooibos, and a hint of dark cacao. It smells like determination softened by warmth.

What's one scent, object, or ritual that reminds you of your inner resilience?

____

____

____

Flavor

Bold. Earthy. Slightly bitter with a sweet undercurrent. It doesn't sugarcoat—it supports. A reminder that strength can be stirred, not forced.

Where in your life are you choosing to show up with strength, even if it doesn't feel easy?

____

____

____

Fill in the blank: I may not feel strong today, but I'm showing up by ____________________________________.

Aftertaste

Lingering warmth. A trace of cacao that stays, like hope after hardship. You've made it this far, and that counts.

What kind of strength are you learning to recognize within yourself now?

____

____

____

Affirmation: I am strong enough for this moment. My strength doesn't need to be loud—it just needs to be real.

SIP 38: A QUIET STEEP

-Eva-

The moment Eva stepped into *The Authenticitea Café*, the weight of the day settled into her bones. It clung to her, not as exhaustion, but as something more delicate, more sacred. A kind of lingering presence, as if she were still standing in that hospital delivery room, watching life arrive in real time.

She had rushed from work the moment she got the call, her heart pounding against her ribs as she sped toward the hospital. Her brother's voice had been laced with excitement and urgency: *It's happening. Now.* She hadn't hesitated, she grabbed her bag, ignored the half-read email on her screen, and drove, barely believing she was about to witness something so profound.

And then, there she was.

She had barely caught her breath when she stepped into the delivery room, just as her sister-in-law pushed through the final moments of labor.

She had braced herself for the expected anticipating the moment the doctor would announce the birth of the baby they'd been preparing for, the one whose name had already been chosen, whose tiny sneakers had already been lined up in the nursery.

Standing at the edge of the delivery room, her breath caught in her throat as the doctor's voice rang out:

"It's a girl!"

A girl.

The entire family had been expecting a boy. Every ultrasound had said so. The baby shower had been filled with shades of blue. The name, the tiny jerseys, the *everything* had been chosen for a boy.

Her brother, who had joked endlessly about finally having a boy in their family full of girls, stood frozen. He had imagined teaching his son to throw a football, had already bought tiny sneakers in blue and white.

But life had a way of surprising you.

Eva turned toward him, waiting for his reaction. The shock on his face was instant, raw. But then, it melted into something softer. Something reverent. He leaned over his wife, whispering something only she could hear, and then he was holding his daughter.

A daughter neither of them had planned for, but one they were already loving in a way that rewrote everything they thought they knew.

Even now, as Eva sat in the café, she could still feel the moment pressing against her skin. The sheer force of it. The quiet, unspoken reminder that no matter how much you prepare, no matter how certain you are of what's ahead, life will always, *always* find a way to surprise you.

And then she noticed something—

For once, she wasn't thinking ahead.

She had been here before, many times, in fact, but today felt different. She wasn't here to work, to plan, to prepare for the next thing.

This birth, her being invited to witness it, had been the *next* big thing.

But for once, right now, in this moment, there was no next.

Her to-do list was checked off, her goals met, her schedule perfectly organized. But instead of relief, a strange restlessness sat in her chest, as if she had lost her footing in the absence of forward motion.

She had spent so much of her life moving forward, always anticipating the next step, her own, someone else's, the path unfolding ahead like a carefully plotted map. There had always been a *next* to prepare for.

The Barista placed a cup of tea in front of her without a word. Just a knowing glance, a quiet moment exchanged. Eva smiled faintly and reached for it, the warmth steadying her hands.

The scent rose to meet her, soft notes of lavender, lemon balm, and vanilla mingled with something deeper, like earth after rain. *The Stillwater Blend.* A tea crafted for quiet moments, for the kind of pause that doesn't demand but simply invites. It was the kind of blend that didn't rush to impress, it unfolded slowly, gently, like exhaling tension you didn't know you were holding.

A folded napkin rested beside the saucer. She traced the edges before unfolding it, reading the handwritten words:

Stillness.

She let out a breath, her fingers pressing lightly against the napkin.

She had always been moving, reaching for or anticipating the next thing, always looking for the next answer, the next challenge. But now, here in this café, with the scent of steeping tea and honey wrapping around her, she didn't *need* to do anything.

And for the first time in a long time, that felt good.

She wrapped her hands around the cup, its heat grounding her. The scent of chamomile, lavender, and honey drifted upward, filling the space between thoughts.

She took a slow sip.

Not thinking about what's next.

Just letting herself be.

"Eva?"

She blinked, pulled from the quiet moment by a familiar voice. Looking up, she saw Hayleigh standing beside her table, a travel-worn bag slung over her shoulder and suitcase in tow, her expression one of warm surprise.

"Hayleigh?" Eva straightened in her seat. "You're back?"

"I've been here for a few days," Hayleigh said, setting her bag down and slipping into the chair across from her. "Figured I'd stop by here on my way out." She glanced at Eva's cup. "Looks like you're in the middle of something."

Eva exhaled, offering a small smile. "Sort of. Just... adjusting to stillness."

Hayleigh chuckled, shaking her head. "That's funny. After weeks of constant movement, I was thinking I could use a little more of it. Maybe we should trade lives for a bit."

Eva let out a quiet laugh, feeling some of the weight in her chest loosen. "Maybe." She hesitated. "But I think I'm finally realizing that I don't always have to be moving forward to be moving at all."

Hayleigh nodded, watching Eva stir the tea that had just been placed in front of her. "That's a good realization. One I think I'm still learning, too."

They sat there in a shared pause, the café humming around them, the scent of tea and quiet understanding settling between them.

Hayleigh glanced at her watch and sighed. “Well, stillness is going to have to wait a little longer for me. I’m actually heading to the airport, off to the next stop.”

Eva tilted her head. “Already?”

Hayleigh smiled, a mix of excitement and exhaustion flickering across her face. “Yeah. Just a quick visit home to reset. Now it’s back to the unknown.”

Eva nodded, understanding in a way she hadn’t before. “Safe travels, Hayleigh.”

Hayleigh stood, slinging her bag over her shoulder. “And enjoy the stillness while you’ve got it.” She grinned. “I’ll have to hear all about what you discover next time I’m back.”

As Hayleigh disappeared through the café doors, Eva stared down at her cup, the warmth still lingering against her palms.

For once, she wasn’t envious of the next adventure.

She relished the stillness, letting it settle in a way it never had before. Some moments aren’t meant to be planned. They simply arrived.

A Taste of Spacious Clarity

When everything else fades

— Inspired by Stillwater Blend: Chamomile, Lavender & Wildflower Honey —

Mood Pairing: For when you long to feel the moment, but need it to approach gently.

Steep Time: Unhurried. Let the stillness settle as deeply as the breath you've been meaning to take.

Body: Soft and serene. A floral hush layered with gentle sweetness.

Origin: Brewed in retreat. Best sipped when the world feels too loud.

Color and Clarity

A pale golden brew, like light caught in silence. It's soft, not showy, and entirely enough.

Where in your life do you need a little more space to simply be?

____

____

____

Aroma

Chamomile and lavender wrap around each other like a lullaby. The honey? Just enough to warm the edges.

What aroma or moment helps you drop into stillness?

____

____

____

Flavor

Delicate floral notes with a grounding sweetness. It doesn't rush, it rests.

What would it feel like to be fully here, without needing to solve or shift anything?

____

____

____

Fill in the blank: In this still moment, I remember ________________.

Aftertaste

Lingering peace. Releasing a breath you didn't notice you were holding. And in that exhale, the permission to slow down.

How can you carry this quiet into what comes next?

____

____

____

Affirmation: I honor the pause. I steep slowly. I trust what stillness reveals.

COME AGAIN

The scent of steeped herbs lingered in the air as the last guest of the evening pushed their chair back, fingers tracing the rim of a half-empty cup. The Barista moved quietly, wiping down the counter, watching as the candlelight flickered against the shop's old wooden beams.

The door jingled softly as the last guest stepped out, pausing just long enough to breathe in the night air. A faint smile on their lips. Another story steeping. Another journey unfolding.

The Barista exhaled, gazing toward the door where the golden light from the streetlamps spilled onto the worn welcome mat. The night was quiet now, the café settling into itself, waiting.

Because that's what *The Authenticitea Café* did. It waited.

For the next traveler. The next seeker. The next soul in need of a moment to pause.

Some would return, drawn back by a whisper of curiosity, the memory of a story they had yet to finish. Others would find their way in for the first time, stepping across the threshold when they least expected it but most needed it.

And somewhere, beyond the clinking of teacups and the scent of honey and herbs, stories continued to steep, waiting for the right moment to be shared.

The Barista smiled to themselves, flipping open a well-worn notebook. They ran their fingers over the edges of its pages, then picked up a pen. With a knowing touch, they wrote:

"There are more stories to tell."

"There is always more tea to pour."

"And the door is always open."

A SIP TO GO

-For You, Dear Reader-

Every cup of tea tells a story, just as every life holds moments of transformation, waiting to be steeped in reflection.

Perhaps, as you've read these stories, you've seen glimpses of your own challenges faced, lessons learned, joys rediscovered. The experiences that have shaped you, the moments that have tested you, and the quiet joys that have warmed you. Each of them matters.

And just as every tea blend is unique, so too is the path you are walking.

So, I leave you with this:

Keep asking questions.
Keep embracing new flavors.
Keep showing up for yourself.

And if ever you need a moment to pause, to reflect, to sip slowly and listen to the wisdom that stirs within, you will always find *A Cup of Authenticitea* waiting for you at *The Authenticitea Café.*

From my cup to yours,

The Authenticitea Barista

BEHIND THE SIPS

-The Author-

Growing up, I always knew I wanted to write a book.

Not just any book, but one that shared pieces of my story, the lessons I've gathered, and the reflections that have shaped me.

What I didn't expect was that this story would unfold in a tea café, through quiet conversations, slow realizations, and a cup of something warm in hand.

Just like life, this book has gone through several pivots. At first, I didn't know what form it would take. I tried on different genres, different voices.

In the end, it became a blend of what I love most, historical imagination, quiet transformation, and the soulful invitation of self-discovery.

Tea was never the plan. But it was always present.

As I paid more attention to my energy and the rhythms that brought me home to myself, I noticed tea kept showing up. It wasn't always about the drink, it was the pause it offered. The quiet. The breath between sips.

And as I wrote, a new voice began to emerge.

Someone pouring tea.

Speaking gently.

Asking questions without expecting an immediate answer.

Holding space rather than taking it.

That's when I introduced *The Authenticitea Barista*.

A familiar presence who poured more than tea; someone who offered wisdom, patience, and just enough pause to let clarity rise to the surface.

Naturally, that led to questions:

Who is The Barista?

What's their story?

How do they always seem to know what to say or do?

The truth is, when I first began writing Authenticitea recipes, I called myself *The Authenticitea Barista*, a reminder to keep it real with myself and others. But when the book began to take shape, I chose not to give The Barista a fixed identity.

No name.

No gender.

No single backstory.

Why?

Because I want The Barista to be *yours*.

A steady presence. A wise friend. Someone who reminds you who you are, without ever needing to explain it.

Maybe for you, *The Authenticitea Barista* is a mentor, a neighbor, a parent, or a friend who knows how to show up with just the right words. Maybe they remind you of someone who held space for you when you couldn't quite hold it for yourself.

They are whoever you need them to be.

A mirror.

A guide.

A quiet kind of knowing.

They don't rush your progress, reminding you that things reveal themselves in their own time.

That's how I approached writing this book, too.

This collection was written the way I live life: Reflective. Imaginative. Open to change.

Some Sips showed up fully formed. Others arrived only after steeping slowly in the background of my life. But each of them eventually revealed themselves, when the timing was right.

Like a good cup of tea, each story needed space.

Stillness.

Intention.

I hope these pages offered you warmth, clarity, and companionship, a reminder that you don't have to figure it all out to keep going.

That even the most ordinary moments can hold insight.

And that your voice, your presence, your truth, are worth sitting with.

TO MY AUTHENTICITEA BARISTAS

–The ones who poured into me over the years–

To my mom and dad –

Thank you for allowing space for me to become who I am. You didn't always need words, your actions said it all. You showed up, supported me, and rooted for me every step of the way.

To my brothers –

Yes, you drove me crazy (as brothers do), but you also gave me space to be myself while keeping a watchful, protective eye. Thank you for showing love in your special way, always.

To my nieces and nephews –

Becoming an aunt has been one of the most joyful and unexpected gifts of my life. It introduced me to one of the purest forms of love, one that's deep, unconditional, and full of wonder. Watching you grow and celebrating the unique ways you each show up in the world inspires me to keep showing up as the best version of myself. Thank you for that.

To my extended family –

My upbringing wouldn't have been the same without all of you. The authentic love that shaped me came from every direction, from aunts, uncles, and cousins who sometimes knew me better than I knew myself. To be known and loved so deeply, as if I were one of your own children or a sibling, is something I will never take for granted.

To my partner (my Love!) –

Thank you for pouring into me with your trust, belief, and constant encouragement. Your support of my work and my ever changing passion projects, especially in this author era, means everything. Thank you for helping bring this dream to life.

To my friends and community –

Thank you for listening to every wild idea, every evolving version of this book, and every "what if." Your reflections, reminders of my strengths, and unwavering support have helped me keep going. You've helped me remember who I am.

And to you, dear reader –

Thank you for being here. Thank you for sipping alongside me. Sharing this experience with you has been one of the most fulfilling pours of my life.

ABOUT THE AUTHOR

-Christina Owens, M.ED.-

Christina Owens is a seeker of life's many discoveries. With Oklahoma in her heart and Virginia beneath her feet, she carries both places as home. One grounding her beginnings, the other shaping her becoming.

She lives a multi-passionate life, with a 20+ year career in education while also earning credentials in real estate, group fitness, and coaching. For her, every experience is an opportunity to explore, reflect, and uncover meaningful insight.

Amid these explorations, tea time has become a cherished practice; a moment to pause that invites curiosity, deepens reflection, and allows discoveries to steep in their own time. Whether journaling in solitude or sharing a cup with others, tea has become a natural part of her reflections and connections.

Christina has spent years curating spaces for meaningful conversation, guiding individuals toward greater self-awareness and authenticity. She believes that discovery is a lifelong process, one best approached with openness, presence, and a willingness to step into the unknown.

When she's not crafting new ways to inspire curiosity, Christina can be found sipping a warm or iced cup of tea, spending quality time with her partner, immersing herself in a good book, whether reading or listening, or indulging in the many activities that bring her joy.

Stay connected:
Website: www.StinaGene.com

A MOOD-BASED GUIDE

–Steep What You Need–

For Stillness & Inner Reflection

When you crave quiet, grounding, or gentle presence.

Sip 1 – A Sip of Presence *(Alora)*

Sip 6 – A Sip of Still Believing *(Faith)*

Sip 13 – *A Sip of the Long Pour (Sara)*

Sip 17 – A Sip of Stillness *(Serena)*

Sip 28 – *A Sip of Gentle Acceptance (Paige)*

Sip 38 – *A Sip of Spacious Clarity (Eva)*

For Courage & Bold Becoming

When you need strength, momentum, or a nudge forward.

Sip 3 – *A Sip of Wild Wonder* (*Allison*)

Sip 7 – *A Sip of Brave Momentum* (*Coach Roberts*)

Sip 12 – A Sip of Courage (*Matthew*)

Sip 14 – *A Sip of Blooming Late* (*Zack*)

Sip 30 – A Sip of the Storm (*Dr. Taylor*)

Sip 36 – A Sip of Not Yet (*Quinton*)

For Healing, Grief & Soft Recovery

When you're tending to loss, letting go, or learning to feel again.

Sip 24 – A Sip of Soft Beginnings (*June & Mike*)

Sip 25 – A Sip of Mending Light (*Jordan*)

Sip 26 – A Sip of Second Chances (*Lucy*)

Sip 34 – A Sip of Truth (*Erica*)

Sip 21 – A Sip of Remembrance (*Elaine*)

For Identity, Self-Worth & Expression

When you're reclaiming who you are or how you show up.

Sip 4 – A Sip of Sovereignty (*Indie*)

Sip 5 – A Sip of True Brew (*Aria*)

Sip 10 – A Sip of Becoming (*Brittany*)

Sip 11 – A Sip of Self-Honoring (*Charlotte & Sterling*)

Sip 31 – *A Sip of Golden Presence* (*Aaron*)

Sip 32 – A Sip of Whimsi-Tea (*Kim*)

Sip 37 – A Sip of Self-Worth (*Alexis*)

For Letting Go, Trusting, and Transitions

When you're between chapters, seasons, or identities.

Sip 2 – A Sip of the In-Between (*Autumn*)

Sip 15 – A Sip of Expansion (*Meghan*)

Sip 18 – A Sip of Connection (*Addison & Tracy*)

Sip 29 – A Sip of Transitions (*Lily*)

Sip 33 – A Sip of Enoughness (*Jay & Vi*)

For Legacy, Meaning & Belonging

When you want to reflect on connection, impact, or what endures.

Sip 8 – A Sip of Strength & Shivers (*Briana*)

Sip 9 – A Sip of Wholeness (*Jean*)

Sip 16 – A Sip of Belonging (*Hayleigh*)

Sip 19 – A Sip of Storyteller's Steam (*Joy*)

Sip 20 – A Sip of the Richer Pour (*Victoria*)

Sip 22 – A Sip of Still-Connected (*Maggie*)

Sip 23 – A Sip of Steady Presence (*Kevin*)

Sip 35 – A Sip of Legacy (*Langston*)

A GLOSSARY OF LEAVES, ROOTS, AND FEELINGS

-what's in the cup -

For those who love to know what they're sipping. A guide to the leaves, blooms, and brews that flavor each sip.

Black Tea

Bold. Deep. Rooted in ritual.
Full-bodied and rich, black tea offers the strength to hold what's heavy and the warmth to soften what's hard. It's the brew of grounding truths, resilience, and quiet confidence.

Butterfly Pea Flower

Blue. Magical. Transformation in a cup.
This vibrant bloom changes color when citrus is added. It's a visual metaphor for growth and possibility—reminding us that change can be beautiful, even before it makes sense.

Calendula

Golden. Gentle. Healing from the inside out.
With its bright petals and subtle floral notes, calendula symbolizes trust, warmth, and quiet recovery. It brings brightness to a blend and calm to the spirit.

Chamomile

Soothing. Soft. A floral exhale.
This gentle flower calms the nervous system and invites stillness.

Chamomile is like a warm blanket at the end of a long day—perfect for reflection, release, and rest.

Chai (Masala Chai)

Spiced. Bold. A brew that carries stories.
A rich blend of black tea and warming spices like cinnamon, cardamom, ginger, and cloves. Chai awakens while it comforts, grounding you in presence with every bold, layered sip.

Cinnamon

Spiced. Sweet. A cozy backbone.
Cinnamon brings warmth, depth, and familiarity to a cup. It's a memory-evoking spice—present in moments of both comfort and change.

Dandelion Root (Roasted)

Earthy. Releasing. Strength in letting go.
Often used for detox and renewal, roasted dandelion root holds the energy of clearing old stories and grounding into what matters now.

Earl Grey

Bright. Elegant. A twist on tradition.
A black tea flavored with oil of bergamot, a citrus fruit that adds a subtle floral sharpness. It's often associated with clarity, refinement, and emotional presence.

Elderberry

Dark. Steady. A quiet shield.
Known for its immune-boosting properties, elderberry brings a grounding sweetness with a touch of tart. It's the kind of support that doesn't make a fuss—but never lets you down.

Ginger

Warming. Fierce. The spark of courage.
Ginger adds bold heat and bright clarity. It stirs energy when you're tired and encourages strength when you feel hesitant—like a nudge to take the next step.

Ginseng

Reviving. Rooted. Quiet endurance.
Traditionally used for stamina and balance, ginseng helps sustain energy and mental clarity—offering a boost that's steady, not sharp.

Green Tea

Fresh. Awakening. A sip of spring.
Delicate and grassy, green tea invites alertness and renewal. It holds the energy of new beginnings—bright, hopeful, and open to what's next.

Hibiscus

Vibrant. Tart. A bold exhale.
Deep crimson in color, hibiscus adds tang and intensity to a brew. It's the flavor of letting go—bright, cleansing, and emotionally expressive.

Honeybush

Warm. Smooth. A softer sibling to rooibos.
Naturally sweet and caffeine-free, honeybush brings comfort without heaviness. It's gentle support for the heart—especially when healing quietly.

Lavender

Calming. Clean. A floral lullaby.
Lavender eases tension and opens the breath. In tea, it settles the nervous system and invites introspection—perfect for unwinding, forgiving, and listening inward.

Lemon Balm

Bright. Reassuring. A balm for busy thoughts.
Used to ease stress and mental fog, lemon balm brings a hint of citrus and clarity to a blend. It's like a deep breath disguised as a leaf.

Licorice Root

Sweet. Stabilizing. Strength in softness.
With a natural lingering sweetness, licorice root soothes the

throat and nervous system. A gentle reminder that tenderness can be powerful.

Linden Flower

Gentle. Heart-opening. Nervous system's hug.
Traditionally used to reduce anxiety and support the heart, linden flower brings peace to tension and grace to the moment.

Oolong Tea

In-between. Evolving. A dance of contradiction.
Sitting between green and black teas, oolong is nuanced and ever-changing. It's the flavor of transition—layered, curious, and always unfolding.

Orange Peel / Citrus

Bright. Lifting. Sunshine in a sip.
Citrus notes add a sparkle to blends—refreshing the spirit and waking up the senses. Perfect for moments of clarity, expression, or emotional reset.

Peppermint

Cooling. Crisp. Mental clarity in a leaf.
Peppermint refreshes and re-centers. It clears cluttered thoughts and brings energetic lift—like stepping outside for a breath of fresh air.

Rooibos

Earthy. Naturally sweet. Steady and strong.
A caffeine-free tea from South Africa, rooibos brews rich and red. It's grounding without heaviness and sweet without trying too hard—like emotional steadiness in a cup.

Rose Petals

Soft. Romantic. The scent of memory.
Rose petals in tea evoke tenderness, beauty, and heart-centered reflection. They're often used to open emotional pathways gently and lovingly.

Sage

Earthy. Ancestral. Quiet power.
Sage adds grounding and wisdom to a blend. Long associated with cleansing and clarity, it supports inner strength and intentional release.

Turmeric

Golden. Bold. Inner fire and healing.
Known for its anti-inflammatory properties, turmeric adds depth and warmth. A reminder that healing can be both fierce and illuminating.

Vanilla Bean

Smooth. Sweet. The taste of tenderness.
Vanilla rounds out sharper notes and lingers with subtle warmth. It softens blends and moments alike—inviting comfort, memory, and a slower pace.

White Tea (Silver Needle)

Subtle. Quiet. A beginning in bloom.
White tea is made from the youngest buds of the tea plant and is the least processed of all teas. It's a tea that invites stillness — perfect for those first moments of clarity that don't demand attention.

www.ingramcontent.com/pod-product-compliance
Lightning Source LLC
Chambersburg PA
CBHW020913310726
48980CB00011B/872/J

* 9 7 9 8 9 9 9 0 2 6 3 0 9 *